PEOPLE CALLED
MUMBAI

Curated by
Nisha Nair-Gupta

First published in India in 2015 by:
Design [Variable]
design.variable@gmail.com

Copyright © 2015 Design [Variable]

First published in 2015
Second Impression 2015

Print Book ISBN: 9789384439255

Design [Variable] asserts the moral right to be identified as the author of this work.

Typeset in Adobe Garamond Pro by Ram Das Lal, New Delhi (NCR)
Printed and bound at
Saurabh Printers
Okhla, New Delhi

Publishing facilitation: AuthorsUpFront

*Dedicated to Mumbai:
the city, the life and the stories!*

Acknowledgements

In the chronology of my work on this book, I would first like to thank Nishita Pereira, who helped all of us brush up on our journalistic skills and grammar.

The project would have been absolutely nothing but for the enthusiastic bunch of authors who were inspired enough to translate their experiences into words: Caleb Pereira, Ipshita Karmakar, Krupa Shah, Mariel Drego, Qurratulain Contractor, Sachi Mavinkurve, Vanessa Lobo...take centre stage!

The best core team one could hope to work with: Aarsha Raveendran, Sahil Dagli, Saman Quraishi and Arundhati Kumar—for persevering and putting in hours of writing, designing and editing. Sahil deserves a special mention for the cover design and book graphics. Moreover, for sharing the belief and excitement and their help in charting the journey of the project.

Our editing and publishing team: Manish Purohit, Arpita Das, Ramya Sarma and Nishtha Vadehra, who made the post-writing part of the work a cakewalk. Their enthusiasm has been motivating and reassuring.

And a vote of thanks to the support and review system: Tarun Gupta, Reshmi Pillai, Anand Gupta, Soumya Kannan, Madhavi Desai and Sujit Pillai.

Finally, a thank you from the team to: Jaya Nair, Prabhakaran Nair, Anita Gupta, Krishna Pillai, Varun Gupta, Vinit Nikumbh, Mohini Freya Dutta, Anuj Daga, Sohan Tari, Awni Patni, Sabahat Fadra, Prayas Abhinav, Aneev Ansari, Ankur Parashar, Aamir Khan, Dolin Golechha, Zankar Gupte, Tabrez Koradia, Burhan Patel, Anas Lakdawala, Wasif Sheikh, Mehernosh Nagporewalla, Hatim Vagher Pandi, Mohammed Arsi, Alisager Talib, Rajiv, Kiran, Kaushal, Pramod, Rattan, Iqbal, Manish, Vijay, Jahangir, Namdev, Ajay, Fatema Kabir, Minaz Ansari, Ronnie Lobo, Martha Lobo, Daryl Lobo, Disha Shah, Atul Shah, Chandresh Shah, Neeta Shah, Kalpana Shah, Nisha Suess, Jaya Navindevi, Priya Subramanian, Pushpa Subramanian, Sayyed Abdul Tawab, Aziz Bhai, Bhikshu Morita, Silin Hu, Sadashiv Kamble, Sambhaji Limbaji Jadhav, Parvez Patel, Parvez Irani, Jabbar Singh, Annubhai, Zeenat Damad, Parvez Ahmed Damad, Jeffrey Amanna, Lesian John, Haresh Ahir, Riddesh Ghadi, Ankita Ashar, Nigel Pereira, Desiree Pereira, Priti Dagli, Samir Dagli, Hiral Gada, Shreyansh Lunkad and Nikhil Jhangiani.

Contents

Introduction

"It was the plague of the 1920s when my grandfather decided to leave Silvassa as a young boy, I think. He came to live with his uncle in Aarey Colony in Goregaon, which he told me, was a hunting ground for the 'whites'. He settled in this little adivasi hamlet after his marriage to my grandma, who was his uncle's niece. Many of his other relatives had also fled to here," says Deepak Varthe, fondly called Deepakbhai, sipping his daily dose of cutting chai at the Juhu studio.

"Somehow our village life has continued till today. People are getting educated, have better opportunities, so not many want to lead our Warli way of life. Though we have our own transport, we are still disconnected from the city. Also the rate at which Aarey Colony's fringes are getting eaten up, we know we will be facing threats of rehabilitation soon. And look at my young daughters— they want to live in buildings!" Spotting his boss walking towards the car, he apologises and promises to continue the conversation another time. Folding his half-read newspaper, he quickly waves goodbye to his friends—the watchman and a sevpuriwala—and settles into the driver's seat.

1

Deepakbhai's story is one of the many discussed in **People Called Mumbai**. Back from a day of exhaustive site visits across the city and conversations with many Mumbaikars, our young interns share their experiences of tracing connections between their stories and the city's own story. Their task has been to map Mumbai through personal narratives, through its humanity. After all, what makes it Mumbai is the people!

With a diverse and ever-growing population, every person who makes the city a home is a story in their own right, often a full-fledged novel. But the story is not theirs alone. It belongs to a collective narrative, falling into compartments that make up the city's history. It is in this context that **Design [Variable]**, an architectural studio, has conducted its first publication project, **People Called Mumbai**.

The stories were found all over the city, some at railway stations, busy markets, plush malls and office lobbies, others from morning walks at parks, underground cafés, forgotten temples and bylanes of the old city, and a few in quiet living rooms. Every conversation began with the question: "How did you come to Mumbai?" And the answer, in each case, an exciting account of a life. This became the background score to most stories, orchestrating a journey of arriving in the city and sometimes, arriving at oneself.

Each story tries to understand an immeasurable parameter of the city: aspiration, conflict, joy, angst, success, struggle, belief, tradition, negotiation, shift, routine and more. Cutting across geography and social divides, detailed with snippets, the stories provide a re-reading of the metropolis.

What would you call this: a short story collection? An

anthology of people? Or an ethnographic map? Essentially, it is a response to the facelessness experienced in the sea that is a metropolis. In the life of a preoccupied citizen there are seldom moments of pause, time to reflect on and take in one's immediate surroundings.

People Called Mumbai dives into this sea of people, surfacing with their stories—a photographer at Juhu Chowpatty doubles as a lifeguard, a successful businessman from Bhuleshwar, a once stranded tourist now rides horse carriages, a migrant who runs the city's only Tibetan restaurant, an artist on the pavements of Kala Ghoda, a Japanese Buddhist monk, Jeeniben relaxing on a cot at Kumbharwada, an unusual social activist operating at a *mela* near Nariman Point, or a Brazilian martial arts expert.... You may have already heard of Indresh Singh, who sells grain at the Dadar *kabutarkhana*, or Navin Rathod, the famous "duplicate" or even Sikander Shah, who sings *qawwalis* every Thursday at Haji Ali Dargah. Each has a unique story; each is a hero.

This book is unique also because of the experiences it offered to the 10 of us, as authors. Engaging with the 55 stories we collected has not been just a literary experience, but a forging of relationships with the people who talked to us. Some lives inspired us beyond words, some brought joy and some moved us. Many people whose names may not have made it to the final print, are still memorable for the conversations we had with them. We often sat in front of our keypads starstruck by these so-called "ordinary" lives, searching for the right words to tell their wonderful tales.

At the end of our exercise—a compilation of experiences rather than a comprehensive catalogue—we came to no single conclusion.

3

But as practitioners of the built environment, it sensitised us, allowing us to experience and engage with life around us. And it definitely brought us closer to the city.

This book is an attempt to share those experiences.

Nisha Nair-Gupta
Curator

A tale of two ticket*wallahs*

The last two decades have seen new trends in movies and movie-goers in Mumbai. The days of weekend shows being sold out on a Wednesday morning, hundreds lining up at cinema box office windows, have given way to instant online booking. Newer forms of entertainment available in the city, together with the spate of new multiplexes, have resulted in audiences at the old single-screen cinemas that once dotted the city, to steadily dwindle. The G7 theatre complex in Bandra, better known as "Gaiety-Galaxy", is a set of seven small theatres and one of Mumbai's first multiplexes, built in the 1970s.

Abdul Rahim stands outside G7 in the heat, alert and ready to rush out to every person stepping out of a rickshaw near the theatre gates. He is the scruffiest of all the black market ticket vendors loitering near the entrance.

"I was introduced to black market ticket selling in 1991, when a friend of mine had a ticket for a movie that he could not watch. He asked me to try to sell it at the theatre," he says. Abdul managed to get Rs 15 for the Rs 4.50 ticket!

Abdul had a flair for sales and saw that the black market could be a good opportunity to make money; it would be far more lucrative than his odd jobs in the catering business. "I came to Mumbai from a village near Silvassa at the age of 15. It was 1988. Initially, I stayed with relatives and worked at restaurants and at a catering company for events and weddings," recalls Abdul, who soon gave up his job and began working his way into the black market ticket sales industry, "full-time".

He started out at Badal Bijli, a cinema hall in Matunga, and worked there for several years. He would typically buy tickets from the box office in advance and then sell them at a higher price to customers on the day of the show. He would befriend the box office ticket salesmen, who would loan him tickets in return for a cut of his profits. Badal Bijli eventually shut down (it was later rebuilt as Star City Cinemas) and Abdul moved from theatre to theatre before settling into black marketeering at the G7 complex.

It is here, across the G7 ticket counter that Abdul often meets Bishwas Pawan, who sits on the other side of the grille. Bishwas is a straight-up senior salesman at the box office counter. He disapproves of Abdul's activities and often scolds him when Abdul asks for a few tickets on loan. "I came to Bombay back in 1967 from Satara, Maharashtra. I found work at construction sites as a labourer. I worked at several sites all over the city before being picked up to work on the construction of a new theatre complex—a novel concept and an ambitious project at that time. Being a film buff, I was excited to be working on the G7 multiplex cinema," says Bishwas.

After the construction work was complete, Bishwas convinced the then owners to allow him to continue working there. He was employed as a janitor at first, but quickly graduated to being an usher, then a ticket collector, and ultimately, a ticket salesman at the box office. Now the senior most among his colleagues, he has worked at the counter for the last 25 years, watching films for free as a bonus. His success allowed him to bring his family to Bombay from Satara 15 years ago and they have lived in Vile Parle ever since.

Abdul, on the other hand, lives in a rented room in Bandra East, close to the station and a short walk away from G7 via a footbridge. The uncertainty of his work is the main reason his family hasn't joined him in Mumbai.

"Twenty years ago movies were advertised through hand-painted hoardings and posters. There was limited information available about a new film, and that created high levels of anticipation among fans. The opening weekend of every new release would be packed, with all shows going house full at every cinema," Bishwas recalls. "Today, with movie trailers forced on us on YouTube, pre-released song videos, interviews and talk-show hype on television, people are able to judge a movie long before its release. While some do well, many films do not even see a full house over the opening weekend." This affects Abdul's business as well.

Abdul knows that the black market ticket industry is dying. Without the crowds and the anticipation around every new release, his profits are limited—while he once managed about Rs 300 per day, he now gets about half of that. He cannot charge too much for a ticket, even if it is in demand, because those who could afford his high prices a few years ago now go to upmarket multiplexes and not to G7. He needs to keep his profit margins low to be competitive and manages to reap good profits only around Diwali, Eid and summer holidays, when more movies are released and the number of patrons is greater.

Citing an incident from 20 years ago, he says, "A large man, probably some bigshot's bodyguard, or maybe just an over zealous cinema-loving goon, once held a gun to my side and threatened me, just for a ticket!" It may sound far-fetched today, but as Abdul says, back then it was not so surprising.

Now the only real threat of physical harm is from the police, who occasionally come by the theatre brandishing *lathis*. The black market ticket vendors run away at their mere sight. Those who do not escape fast enough get beaten. "There is no bribery," Abdul claims. "We don't make enough profits for that anymore and the police know it."

Bishwas, who does not like violence in life or onscreen, misses the genre of comedy films in Bollywood. No one makes those now. "Tastes and preferences have changed," he says. "Now people prefer action films with lots of special effects."

His love for films has a lot to do with his loyalty to the G7 complex. Sitting behind the grille of the box office window, leaning back comfortably in his chair, he reminisces about bygone years, when films were everyone's favourite source of entertainment, the fans and the queues at his counter, the anticipation and the excitement!

Though its crowds have reduced greatly, today G7 is one of the few places left in the city where there are still traces of the animation and euphoria of old, as people whistle and dance in the aisles as a dance number from a super-hit film plays onscreen.

These remnants of a fading Bollywood fan culture keep both these ticket salesmen—each so different from the other—going. Bishwas gets a bit of the excitement and joy he craves, while Abdul ekes out a living from it for as long as he can.

Towers of silence

Qissa-i-Sajan begins from the Great Khorasan and recounts the tale of the emigration of Zoroastrian Parsis from Iran to the western part of Gujarat, ending with the establishment of a fire temple at Sanjan. One can only imagine a group of Iranians fleeing the overbearing Arabic forces, braving storms and sheer exhaustion to finally enter India and settling down as an independent community. In time, with the establishment of various businesses in Mumbai under the East India Company, the Parsis from Gujarat found their way to prosperity and glory with their mercantile activities and set up base in the northern part of Mumbai.

Today, despite their dwindling numbers, Parsis still seem to be finding their way. Many look like they live in a bygone era, their fists clenched tight, in the hope that the threads of their history don't slip away from them. They live in tightly knit communities and are said to revel in their own isolation. It was to dispel this notion that I visited the sky burial place of the Parsi dead, the Tower of Silence on Malabar Hill.

"Only Parsis allowed here." These words greet me as I enter the premises. There is a courtyard of sorts, surrounded by sprawling Victorian-style cottages with a desolate air. The approach to the office is a climb away from the hustle and bustle of the blaring traffic towards the quiet, solemn environs of a tree-covered hillock. In these picturesque surroundings stands the caretaker, in a white flowing *kurta* and a red velvet skull cap, admonishing me for seeking information about a place that is essentially for the dead.

"There are five *dokhmas* in this place. I am the hearse driver, but I will show you around," says Uncle, who wears a white *ganji* and *pajama* pants and has a dignified, business-like demeanour. I am led to the miniature model of the Tower of Silence, which is a circular pit with designated places for the corpses. "There are three concentric circles surrounding the pit. The outer one is for men, the inner circle is for women, and the smallest one for the corpses of children," he says in a gruff tone. "The vultures are natural scavengers and within 15 minutes, the flesh is wiped clean of the bones. The bones are then dropped in the circular pit, from where we clear them and bury them elsewhere."

There is no sentimentality attached to this job; bodies are referred to straightforwardly and the *dokhma* is treated as what it is: a disposal pit. This stems from a basic belief in the absolutes of "purity" and "pollution" in Zoroastrianism—the corpse is the ultimate example of corruption and pollution; it would be heinous to bury it and spread its pollution to the three elements of Earth, Fire and Water.

"The aim of life is to give back. The Parsi, even in his death, performs the ultimate charity, which is offering one's body to the vultures as food. Burial would lead to the putrefaction and corruption of the Earth, which we revere," says Uncle, even as we watch a funeral procession going by, and vultures hovering above in the sky.

After complaints by the residents of Malabar Hill about the vultures dropping parts of the dead over residential spaces, solar panels were installed to speed up decomposition of the bodies. "There are a number of people working in the establishment—pall bearers, hearse drivers, priests, management and so on—all paid and all Parsis." These men perform the sacred dance of death, beginning with the hearse driver who carries in the dead from the hospitals, the priest who consecrates the place, the pall bearer who takes the dead to the designated spot where the families are asked to bid adieu, the people who ultimately transfer the body into the *dokhma*, and finally the vultures, who strip the corporeal body while the sun reduces the bones to dust.

"I live in Parel, very close to the hospitals," the hearse driver chuckles. It may sound jarring to us, but constantly being around the dead desensitises a person, enough to actually make jokes. According to the scriptures, the Zoroastrian way of disposing of the dead is the most scientific method, as it does not pollute nature, nor does it allow the corpse to spread its diseases to living beings. It makes one wonder why there is so much sentimentality attached to death. What is wrong with going through the rituals without tears, and with happiness for a life well spent? The guide book that is given to me says that in death there are "no epitaphs, no urns. It is just a sensible way to dispose of something which is ultimately meant to decay".

Behind the scenes

"I think I had a talent for captivating an audience. It started with my grandmother telling me old folktales back in my hometown in Orissa. That rubbed off on me. I could keep a person or two mesmerised in a conversation." This is Sukant Panigrahy, one of the acclaimed, new-wave art directors in Bollywood, known for his many radical works. "I was always bold. Perhaps this is what led to the first leg of my youth: activism."

For a few years Sukant dabbled in local politics and gangs, but then his conscience took over. Or perhaps the storyteller in him wanted to explore itself. After a brief stint in Bhubaneswar, he decided to come to Mumbai. "I loved watching TV as a child. Back then, for lack of options, we watched whatever was shown," says Sukant. An avid viewer of mainstream cinema, he realised that maybe one day he could tell his stories through movies.

After a fortnight of ticketless travel, he reached Mumbai in 1994. "The streets of Mumbai were worse than they are now. I had to beg for a job at a small time restaurant and got work as a kitchen scullion." Sukant talks about his life on the streets: "Things turned

13

ugly quite soon. The older men would prey on the younger ones like me." A ragging incident escalated into a rape attempt and soon Sukant was looking for work again.

"This is the film capital of India, and you can't go a long time without trying out as a film set handyman. After finding accommodation in Andheri, with the help of an acquaintance, I started going for set calls—turning up at a set early morning in the hope that the director needs miscellaneous help." His extraordinary ability to adapt to his surroundings came to the fore. "We did anything and everything—sweeping, clearing, carrying heavy equipment, painting, getting coffee ready, taking orders from actors and directors…but I took a special interest in painting. I was supposed to mix paints with water, get them ready for the actual painters. Soon I learned the difference between acrylics and other kinds of paint. Then I tried my hand at a few set painting sessions when ever I was allowed to."

The Bollywood scene in Mumbai in the early 1990s was a fantasy-driven enterprise, with lavish sets, effervescent dance numbers, targeting the semi-rural masses of India—about 70 percent of the country. There was nation-wide hysteria that brought many to the mythical Mumbai. "I slowly learned my way around designing a set while working with Sharmista Roy for many years. Together we did a lot, progressed swiftly. I became an unofficial art director in 1998. I also bought a computer and practiced on whatever new software came up."

It has now been five years since Sukant set up his own enterprise, with a team of architects who design the layouts of the sets, film students, graphic designers and so on. Proud of its exponential growth, he points to trophies sitting on a shelf in his sparsely-furnished bohemian living room. "I've won a few awards for my work, but it's never been about the money. I always wanted to earn a name in the industry and now that I have, I look forward to another part of my life, maybe as an educationist!"

His early years in politics and the struggle and trysts with Bollywood and Mumbai shaped Sukant's approach to his work and life. "When I first came to the city, it was still reeling from the riots of the early 1990s. The people in my building were so racially discriminatory. No one got along, especially the parents." Sukant invited children from his neighbourhood for an art workshop. Around 50 children turned up at his doorstep. "It was fun. I took them around the city to do things they'd always wanted to do. I made them create a wishlist and told them I'd grant at least three of those wishes." His own irascible youth is forgotten as he talks about the pleasures of guiding naughty children like him.

So now it's all about the future. "What I'm looking at now is conceptualising an environmentally-conscious village/town wherever I get the chance, for which around 300 acres of land would be required. I've already talked to a few people about this. I'm thinking of public parks, irrigation canals, organic materials and a research and development centre, along with educational institutes. It's all still in the conceptual phase." Fleshing out details of a project based on similar ideas, Sukant narrates, "After long months of hard work and coordination we are organising a green festival in the small hill station of Matheran. The Matheran Green Festival is envisioned on the ideas of conserving nature, the re-transformation of the environment and green villages. I think it is still just a seed. I hope it will develop and spread across the fields of art, commerce and science. His ideas also stem from his

15

intense criticisms of urban life, concern about migration patterns and excess consumption of mass media.

"For me it's all about what happens at the grassroots level. If that is sorted out, everything is cool. Since India is the land of a million villages, I say we need to improve these units of human resource. I am hardly an authority on planning, but this concern strikes a chord in my heart. Everything else seem very trivial now. I can safely say that films were just an indulgence, perhaps a way to find my true calling. My real passion is to direct all my energies in the betterment of the environment, our environment."

Little things in life

What's Mumbai without the local trains!

Every Mumbaikar may crib and complain about the rush and the lack of breathing space in the locals, and yet they know that these trains form a very special part of their lives. Thousands of people make their way around the city in the local trains and friendships are formed in an instant. While some are seen chatting animatedly with their fellow travellers, there are also those who fidget with their cellphones or tune out the world as they listen to music or read a book. The dreamy ones stare out of the windows, watching the city whizz past.

For a writer, the local train is like an endless conglomeration of stories. Every faceless individual I have come across on these journeys is a different story. One such fascinating tale is Gayatri's. An eight-year-old in a blue dress, her big brown eyes gleaming with curiosity, she sits by the window, gazing at the world outside as it glistens in the afternoon sun. Gayatri is the daughter of Niyati Deshpande, a vendor who sells nail paint, hair clips and hair bands in local trains.

She sits on the seat opposite mine and her broad smile catches my attention. "I love Parle-G! It's my favourite biscuit!" she exclaims as the train rumbles past the Parle-G factory in the suburbs. She rests her arm on the window sill and breathes in the sweet bakery smell that wafts through the air, smiling contentedly. The look of utter delight on Gayatri's face is so endearing that I can't help smiling back at her.

"That ice cream is so pink!" she interrupts my thoughts as she points to a fellow traveller eating strawberry ice cream. "I want a pink-coloured ice cream," she whispers, looking disheartened for a second. The next moment, her eyes brighten up once again. "*Aai* is always busy selling nail paint. She never lets me use any, I don't know why. Do you like nail paint? Would you buy one?" she rattles on. "I don't like travelling by train all day. Everyone comes and goes and I'm always here, going to and fro and still reaching nowhere. I have to be here till *Aai* finishes selling all the nail paint." It's her summer vacation and since she has no school, she accompanies her mother as she goes about her daily trade.

Gayatri has a younger brother, Manish, who is a year old and clings on to his mother in the jostling train. I follow her gaze as she stares at her mother talking to a customer. "My father is a rickshaw driver and he drives in and around Dahisar. We have a house there," she explains with pride.

I ask her about her friends and her face lights up. "Reema is my best friend in the whole world! We play every day in the garden beside our house." From our conversation, I get the sense that Gayatri has very high aspirations. She tells me that she wants to be a teacher when she grows up, which surprises me. Quite a mature decision for a girl her age, I think to myself. But she tells me that she adores and idolises her school teacher. "Geeta Miss is absolutely lovely! And she always gives me a 'good' on my English homework," she says. Unlike many kids of her age, who can be seen selling a variety of things on local trains, Gayatri studies at the municipal school in Dahisar. I think that was very responsible of her parents.

She continues chatting merrily, telling me about her trip to Nagpur to meet her maternal grandparents. Originally from Nagpur, Gayatri's parents moved to Mumbai when they discovered the lack of job opportunities for people like them who had no educational qualifications.

Like any child Gayatri is excited about her birthday, which is coming up in a few months and which she's been planning for months. "I want a maroon dress, exactly like the one Reema wore on her birthday," she tells me. "I've already told Baba and I hope he gets it for me!"

The train halts at a station and a woman selling fish gets on. Gayatri crinkles her nose and makes a face. "I hate fish!"

Her childish complaint reminds me of my days as a child and how, back then, only the little things mattered.

My stop approaches and I get up, not wanting to leave this happy, innocent kid, hoping I'll meet her again. She smiles at me one last time and as I get off the train, she waves at me, one hand flailing in excitement and the other still holding her nose.

The fading *brun maska*

A walk though Churchgate is always delightful. There are buildings left behind by the British, wide roads, open *maidans* and a vibe that that sets it apart from the rest of the city. There is an unavoidable feeling of nostalgia in every street and each building. Then there is the chain of Parsi food joints, which have been there for so long that they're now part of the city's history. Café Military, Ideal Corner, Yazdani Bakery, Kyani's & Co, Britannia & Co and Jimmy Boy, to name a few. They've been serving people wholesome, authentic Parsi food for decades now. Just their names bring up images of *brun maska, dhansak, kheema pav* and *salli boti*. They're more than just eateries, they're a culture, and they're something very dear to the people of Mumbai.

Café Military is one of those iconic Parsi restaurants, delighting people with their food since 1933. In Fort, Café Military has been an escape for office goers, college students and others, for anyone who wants a simple delicious meal topped with their classic custard. The owner, Behram K Khosravi, welcomes customers with a wide grin. He is extremely approachable and affable; it isn't difficult to strike up a conversation with him.

"My father, Khodaram B Golabi, came to India from Zainabad, Iran, in 1925. In those days there wasn't much scope in Iran, so he decided to come to Bombay with my mother to earn a living. They had to go to the police station every 11 months to get their passports checked, till the law eventually became lax and they became a part of the city," says Behram. "My father changed our name from Golabi to Khosravi to avoid any trouble in the future. The city was very different back then. It was nicer. Landlords would willingly sell shops. So my father bought this place and Café Military was born in 1933. My father brought *brun maska,* omelettes and *bhurji,* which weren't made in those days, to Bombay. The place slowly became very popular."

There are few customers in the dimly lit café. The beautifully ornate chairs look like they were crafted in a different era. Everything in the café, from the tiles to the memorabilia on the walls makes it seem frozen in time. A Parsi couple walk in and greet Mr Khosravi, who grins and welcomes them warmly. The fans creaked a little as they cooled the café that had once catered to the British and then to thousands of migrants after Independence. "I took over the café in 1951. I've been managing it ever since. I had to make a few changes to keep the business going. In the 1950s South Indian restaurants became popular in Mumbai and we began to lose customers. Suddenly our famous *brun maska* wasn't enough to keep people coming. That's when we added Mughlai dishes like *kheema pav* to our menu, to attract more customers. We got most of our business back. I expanded quite a bit at that time. I bought land in Dahanu and started growing *chikoo*, coconuts and *jamun*. I supplied fruit to many places. I also own property in many places in the city, like Andheri and Dadar. But I spend most of my time at the café. I help the staff and cut bread for the *brun maska* sometimes," he says. The counter is busy. A waiter emerges from the kitchen with a bottle of raspberry soda (found mostly in Parsi restaurants) and a plate of omelette *pav*.

"Who's going to take over when I'm gone? I don't know…my eldest son takes care of the farms in Dahanu. My son and daughter work in the US. My daughter is a doctor. My granddaughter thinks of Mumbai as a dirty and noisy city. My wife is at home. We're both getting older. I don't know what will happen in the future or who'll take care of this café," he says wistfully.

As time passes, the memorabilia on the wall seem to multiply and the accolades pile up, but the walls themselves are fading. The smell of freshly made bread spreads through the neighbourhood every day. No one knows if the bread will be made tomorrow, or if the doors of the café will be open. Time is passing and the old will be replaced by the new. But will Mumbai ever be the same without raspberry soda and *brun maska*?

Past perfect

It's 2:30 pm on a Monday and it seems to be a very busy afternoon at Vikas Dilawari Architects, a modest office space in Jawahar Nagar, Goregaon West. Owned by Vikas Vedprakash Dilawari, a 48-year-old conservation architect, it is filled with young employees, some busy working on their computers, others taking printouts and a few rushing into the cabin for discussions with the boss. Putting his work aside, he reminisces, "During the 1950s and 1960s my father came to Mumbai from Kashmir to set up his business. Even back in those days Mumbai was considered the city of gold, the land of opportunities and the dreamer's paradise! He established his business here in Goregaon, which was a pleasant neighbourhood, and also bought a house here."

Bracketed on either side of the railway line by the Western Express Highway and Linking Road, Goregaon is primarily a middle-class residential neighbourhood. Until the late 1970s, the suburb was sparsely populated; this began to change with residential localities springing up. "One of our favourite pastimes during our childhood was to play with dragonflies and butterflies. Back in those days, there were no compound walls for buildings, so we friends often spilled out on to the road to play cricket. There were a few *talavs*, and so many trees and birds. Mumbai gave me a beautiful childhood. But slowly, the birds started disappearing; residents started building compounds walls for safety. Then came the car parks in the compound and box windows, grilles, CCTV cameras… and the list goes on. The concept of neighbourhood friends does not even exist anymore," he says with disappointment.

During his school days at Jamnabai Narsee School, Juhu, Vikas Dilawari was fascinated with history. But it was only when he started his graduate diploma in architecture at the LS Raheja School in 1983 that he really discovered the architectural heritage of the city. "Up until then, I hadn't seen many of the heritage buildings," he says. "I had always loved history, so my interest in historical buildings was natural, I suppose." Architecture school introduced him to many of Mumbai's beautiful structures, but it also showed him how little they were appreciated.

"We had an academic exercise where we were supposed to redesign Crawford Market. I wanted to conserve it, but didn't get good marks; people who suggested demolishing it got the best marks. That motivated me to study further and I even did my thesis on it just to prove that I had not been wrong. Hence, I landed up doing conservation, and there's been no looking back since. Back then, conservation involved a lot of activism, because it was not in fashion," says Dilawari.

After he decided that he wanted to specialise in conservation architecture, he enrolled for a masters degree in the subject at the School of Planning and Architecture in New Delhi. In 1990, he was among one of the early batches of Indian students with this specialisation. "When I got my degree, no one knew what it was, because the concept of conservation architecture was introduced in India only in 1985; so some people thought I was doing 'conversation architecture'," he laughs. Back then, heritage buildings didn't offer as much work or pay as other types of architecture. "Working as a conservation architect has definitely involved sacrifices," he says. "You can't make big money, although it is getting more comfortable now. Back then getting small works on the exterior of the building were considered to be a great thing and interior works were out the question. Conservation is not like conventional architecture or interior design; there are no quick projects. During my initial days we used to volunteer with various NGOs to conserve buildings that the government wanted to demolish," he adds.

Between 1985 and 1988, Dilawari began his career with the first heritage conservation project in the country, the Gaiety Theatre project in Shimla, under Ved Segan, the architect of Prithvi Theatre. Since then, Dilawari has actively helped build infrastructure required for conservation architecture, which was near non-existent when he had started working. Perhaps the most important job has been putting together a skilled labour force. "Since conservation demands a lot of skilled manual work, there was a huge requirement for good craftsmen. The difficulty of finding craftsmen who professionally work with traditional materials and deliver good quality of work is a major challenge even today."

In 2001 his restoration of the Rajabai clock tower, built between 1869 and 1878, received a UNESCO Asia Pacific special mention award. A few years later, in 2005, his work on the 140-year-old Bhau Daji Lad Museum in Byculla received an award for excellence—the only building in the city to have received the honour. His portfolio of work also includes an impressive array of other iconic Mumbai structures, including Flora Fountain, Esplanade House, getting CST listed as a World Heritage Site in 2004, Alpaiwala Museum (the only Parsi museum in the world), JN Petit Library, Army Navy Building, Standard Chartered Bank, Lal Chimney Compound or Marzban Colony in Mumbai Central, Royal Bombay Yacht Club residential chambers in Apollo Bunder, and many more. His works have been recognised by UNESCO 10 times, which makes him one of India's topmost conservation architects.

"The field of conservation architecture needs patience and also in-depth knowledge about the history of the building one is working on. It's all about taking the building back to the way it was originally built." His work has often led Vikas Dilawari to travel across the globe. For example, finding the right hue for the Bhau Daji Lad Museum was a particularly time-consuming process. Dilawari visited Victorian heritage buildings in the UK to make sure that the colours he found matched those under the layers of paint, operating much like a detective searching for clues.

The process of sensitising people to the value of heritage is most important and Dilawari is exploring all avenues to help raise the next generation of conservation architects to whom he can pass the baton. He conducts heritage walks as a means of raising awareness. After all, it was through walks in historic areas organised during his college days that he fell in love with historic buildings. "I used to take children from my daughters' school for these walks," he says. "We need to really think about the legacy that we are going to leave behind."

Is it only redevelopment or are we going to preserve our architectural heritage? "My wife says that my future is in 'ruins', but I tell her that 'ruins' are what make an archaeologist happy," he laughs winding up this little conversation before resuming business as usual.

A prolonged holiday

It is impossible to miss the silver coloured, flower decorated and disco lit horse carriages that frequent Marine Drive in the evening. These carriages came to be known as 'Victorias' when Bombay was under Queen Victoria's reign, being an important mode of transport for the Britishers in the old city. In between the *chaiwallas* and the *bhelwallas* wandering through the area, one can often spot Salman Khan driving his Victoria with overwhelmed tourists in the passenger seat.

Salman is dressed in a simple checked shirt, loose trousers and regular flip-flops. When asked to talk about his childhood, he says his memories are blurred. "My parents, my three elder sisters and I came to Bombay by train from Madras on a short vacation. After arriving at Mumbai Central, then called Bombay Central, excited to see the city, we decided to take a short tour of Bombay before checking into our lodge. We took a taxi and visited the Haji Ali and then went to a small dargah near Antop Hill at Wadala."

Salman was barely eight years old, but clearly remembers his first day in Bombay. "While we were at the dargah, peacefully walking around, suddenly there was commotion, people screaming and running everywhere. In the blink of an eye, I saw a group of men holding swords darting towards us. Not knowing what to do and where to go, my parents tried to gather us and run. Before we could break into a sprint, I saw swords slice through my parents and sisters, leaving streams of blood."

Those were the Hindu-Muslim riots of the early 1990s that killed many and changed the lives of many more. "Devastated and clueless about where to go and where not to, I felt uncertain, lost and scared. My mind kept replaying scenes of people collapsing, children crying and women screaming."

Unfortunately, Salman was left alone after the loss of his family. Being a child, all he knew was that he was from Madras. With no access to a telephone, no local guardian and negligible local linguistic skills, he had no choice but to stay in the city. Salman recalls spending days wandering around, searching for food and begging passers-by on footpaths for money.

"I had no idea about what was to come, what I was going to do. Helpless, with nothing to do and nowhere to go, I started looking for places to work as a servant. Someone directed me to a Chinese food stall near Worli, saying that I would get work there. And so I started working at the stall and the owner provided me with food and shelter, along with daily wages."

Staying and working in a city with a diverse mix of religions and languages makes it easier to become a part of it eventually. "I remember how those English-speaking students would converse; it always pinched me since I couldn't finish my formal education. After a few years I started going for tuitions to learn English."

Salman learnt how to speak Hindi, Marathi, Gujarati, English and Malayalam. His multilingual skills inspired him to work as a guide near the Gateway of India. But with limited knowledge of the city, he could merely blabber and draw customers to a particular hotel, for which he would be paid a commission.

"Watching families and tourists at the Gateway reminded me of how I had come with my family, how an event had changed my life, how it had made me grim, vulnerable and angry," he says. He recalls the days when, drunk with the idea of revenge, he turned to darker professions.

"I landed up in jail for my wrongdoings. After spending seven years there I started realising my follies...the difference between right and wrong, Once, I pick-pocketed a man in a crowded bus. When I got down and opened his wallet, I found his salary slip along with his salary, ATM cards, etc. I wondered how his life must be."

But later, feeling ashamed, Salman decided to trace the address in the wallet and return it to the person to whom it belonged. "His family was so happy when they received it. On several occasions they even invited me for family events. I built many relationships— some worked, some didn't. I became more social, met people and made friends with a few who work at the *mela*. Finally, I decided to work at the *mela*. It gives me pleasure to see people happy, families together."

Salman has not only been a victim, but also a victor. He has witnessed so many facets of Mumbai. When asked about his family, Salman smiles. "It's been almost two years since I got married and I now have a daughter who is a month old. I have my own family here with me and I want to do all I can for them!"

About his future plans he says, "I want to take my family to

31

Chennai so that my daughter doesn't get to see the side of Mumbai that I have seen. It seems like a journey that will take me back from where it all began."

Marathon wings

It would be very interesting to map the pattern of migration that results from people getting married. Most women migrate to their husbands' home, town or city of residence. One of many millions of such women is Archana Gupta, who lives in a posh suburb of Mumbai. Jovial and forever smiling, she talks about how she came to the city and about her apprehensions. "I was born and brought up in Jaipur, a relatively small city, in Rajasthan. My maternal grandparents used to work in Mumbai. So I would visit them every year as a child, during holidays and long weekends, and thus was constantly in touch with Mumbai. To be very frank, I used to think that life in Mumbai was very fast-paced and people were constantly running. One should visit Mumbai, but never settle down in the city. But here I am, now steeped in this bullet-paced city. I now find the people in my hometown very lethargic and slow."

Archana finished her graduation in arts and moved to Mumbai after getting married to Yogesh Gupta, a property developer. She had a lot of misgivings about the city, but the process of making it her own turned out to be fairly easy. "It was very difficult to accept at first that I was moving to a place where I had never wanted to be. But when I came here, I got introduced to the discipline and routine of things; I got to understand the lifestyle here. Slowly but steadily I started adapting."

Soon after, Archana devoted her time to raising her sons and being a homemaker. Only after her kids had grown up did she think of making an identity of her own. "We shifted to Vile Parle around eight years ago, and the kind of people around us changed my perceptions about myself and made me more ambitious and proactive. It is only after coming here that I gave any thought to myself and decided to start learning something new.

Vile Parle is one of Mumbai's most prominent suburbs. It serves as the location of the first Parle biscuit factory. It houses Mumbai's Chhatrapati Shivaji International Airport's domestic terminal. While originally Vile Parle consisted of Marathi families, over time the demography of the suburb has changed, with more Gujarati business clans coming in. It has now also become the second major education centre after the Churchgate-to-Charni Road area, with the establishment and growth of a huge educational complex. "The people in this locality are educated and are conscious about their lifestyle. That is primarily why I think I started to restructure myself. It all started with my curiosity to understand what my husband does. I decided to take up a diploma in property management and construction. After 15 years of being a housewife, just so that I could bridge conversation gaps between my husband and me. Now, whenever he has something to say about his business, I can contribute and talk about it with him," Archana says with a self-satisfied and proud smile.

Does she work with her husband? She quickly explains, "Oh no, I don't. I did the course just to understand what my husband is into, to get a fairer idea. I had different dreams and different things to pursue. I took up a year-long course on event management and started my own firm with a partner and now I'm a wedding planner." Traditional Indian weddings include many ceremonies and rituals that are now being mixed with western concepts. Typically, an Indian wedding in the city will mean processions on the roads, lots of dancing and music and fun. But there is more, Archana elaborates. "Many a time people ask me what it is that I want to do with weddings, how I see weddings. I see them as a fusion of two cultures and a merging of not just two people, but of two families and their traditional values. It gives me pleasure to be part of something so important in any two people's lives. I do it because I love doing it."

In a fast moving city like Mumbai it becomes really difficult to plunge into multiple activities, especially for leisure. Most of the time people are either rushing to reach home, stuck in traffic or simply uninspired. Archana has a different take on this—she is an active member of a running group for the Mumbai Marathon, the largest of its kind in Asia and the biggest mass participation sporting event on the continent. It is the richest race in India with a prize pool of USD 350,000.

Shedding light on her hobby she says, "It is all in the mind. I am really passionate about running. Every morning I make sure I get out to run or jog. You can call it my 'me time'. I really can't do without it. I've been running for the Mumbai Marathon that happens in January for the last eight years. We have already started our practice sessions for the next one and we have to start as early as

4 am. But it is a high that I thoroughly enjoy. I'm glad I've inspired my sons to start taking their health and fitness very seriously."

Ask her what else she looks forward to and what other ambitions she has and she smilingly replies, "I am really grateful for the openness of this city, be it the Kala Ghoda Fest, or the organic market in Dadar, or the delicacies of South Mumbai during Ramadan. There are so many things to be done, like tasting different cuisines, taking up social causes, traveling to different corners of the world and much more."

With a grin she folds up her sleeve to reveal a small tattoo of a bird on her forearm. "I went to this artist to get a tattoo. I didn't know what I wanted at first. My tattoo artist took three sittings to understand me as a person and then came up with this image of a dove in flight. I feel like this dove, all set to soar, on the move and ready to fly."

"I think better when I run"

The angry gulls squawk like children who have lost their favourite playground, while free-spirited mongrels loll about, warming their bodies in the sand. But the most interesting species on the beach are the newly-freed Mumbaikars, clowning about in the muddy ebb of the Arabian Sea, flinging hoopla rings towards a row of biscuit packets, flinging themselves on the sand to tackle the guy with the football, jogging like focused athletes or cuddling up to a lover in a little sand burrow.

The artistes near the bordering wall are spectacular in their movements, somersaulting on the spot on the sand, jumping over their friends' hunched frames and doing that special dramatic somersault off the wall. Garth, a fair, pony-tailed and physically fit youth with a wispy moustache grins when a friend unsuccessfully attempts to leap over another's half-crouched body, mistiming the move and careening into the soft sand. "I don't think you've loosened your knees today," he says mockingly. "Go warm up, you lazy bugger."

This is a clique of parkour artists—"free-running", in layman's terms, the art of obstacle-defeating that uses physical elements of the urban environment as stunt-props while running in a straight line. "The parkour artist is seemingly unconcerned about obstacles like walls, tanks, parked cars, etc., and uses these elements by running through or jumping over them instead of navigating around them. The simple philosophy is to travel from point A to point B with the most efficient and fluid locomotion," explains Garth. "It's all about precision jumps. That's how you start. Then you move on to a combination of precision jumps. That's when it gets creative. The city becomes the arena, where we start using the railings, benches, curbs…and imagine what all you can do with it! It's so liberating!"

Garth speaks about his own journey: "I never felt free in a classroom; I'd always score the least marks. So my teachers always had me on their radar. It was a lot of pressure and I began to believe that I was not good enough, or that I was unnaturally stupid." He says that the young East Indian Christian community in Mumbai, which is concentrated in the former fishing hamlets of Malad and Bandra, have been typecast as classroom laggards, with no interest in studying. "But by the time I reached class I had no inkling of many basic concepts. It took me three years just to pass. I lost many friends; some went ahead and some abroad and I felt stuck in a time warp."

Probably an aberrance of education, a general disregard for conformity and the entrapment of the quaint gaothans by the metropolis—all these factors have contributed to the anomalous creativity and professional choices of many young people here. "Most of the youngsters have been bred as potential migrants, not interested in staying in the city or even in finding a grounded Indian identity." Garth believes the condition could stem from the lack of stability that comes from being a minority community.

"My father is in the merchant navy, always away for more than half the year." he says, The older generation went after a peculiar set of overseas jobs that included sailing in the merchant navy, working on oil-rigs and joining the oil rush of the late 1960s in the Gulf, usually in Dubai and Abu Dhabi. "I hated not having him around for such long periods. Mom is a seamstress and wedding cake maker with shops in Orlem and Bandra. Garth was "lost for four years. It was a deep, anti-social, existential crisis. It was a documentary film called *Jump London* that gave me direction and it blew my mind because I had always loved the idea of a ninja. I was always clowning around imagining I was one," says Garth. He joined a parkour group on Facebook, made friends and soon they started their own team called "Free Souls". "We all practiced in a gym for the first six months, to train for a parkour-fit body. Then we started training in different parts of the city—not just the beach, but terraces and playgrounds, any place that was decently safe to practice."

It wasn't easy. "I quickly learned that parkour, more than just an art, was a discipline. And for the first time I actually started waking up to early morning alarms, trained at the gym, built my stamina and did every possible calisthenic exercise, because I used to be really pudgy. My parents tried convincing me to get a basic commerce degree, but I told them I wanted to ride the wave and not be distracted from parkour," says Garth. "They were very disappointed, I remember. That was the worst time for me in the house, because my dad was home and he threatened to kick me out. My sister kept my parents at bay, and convinced them to let me go ahead and see how things went with my discipline."

Garth dreamed of being on television. He dabbled in local youth-oriented programs on MTV and Star that had reality games, as well as the Indian version of Takeshi's Castle, a vaudeville show that invites contestants to get thrown around a ridiculous obstacle course. "Then I got a good break: Free Souls was sponsored for a Parkour meet in Malaysia by a British foundation that teaches it internationally, especially in South Asian countries. We went there and learned so much. Being exposed to an international competition just opened my mind to so many possibilities." As his confidence grew, Garth decided to do a correspondence course in mass media from Wilson College. "I'm in my second year. I also contribute to the family by teaching a parkour class and the money is pretty decent."

"Check this out." He runs towards the sand-kissed beach wall, his feet effortlessly treading the wall as if it was the ground, and does a back-flip in a perfect 360 degree arc, landing on his feet with athletic panache. The free-flowing mechanics of his body are like waves washing against the sandy shore, a rare open space in the city's concrete jungle.

Always have a Plan B

"Dreams are very persistent!" says the woman with near-perfect skin, luscious burgundy hair and a smile that lights up her face. Karen (name changed) was 19 when she realised that she would no longer be able to push aside her dream of becoming a supermodel in the City of Dreams, Mumbai.

"The thrill of walking the ramp with all eyes on you, people staring with awe and envy at the clothes you wear, and seeing your face on posters all around the city—I had dreamed endlessly about that moment, about how perfect my first ramp walk would be!" Karen reminisces.

Mumbai is home to many who aspire to superstardom, who gamble everything on that one chance of being famous. Only five percent find their road to success; the rest spend their lives struggling to find that perfect opportunity. Many from the modelling industry believe that "instant, overnight success" is the mantra. One of those believers is Karen, who belongs to a Christian community in the north-eastern state of Arunachal Pradesh, and idolises Naomi Campbell. "I came to Mumbai two years ago hoping to become a model. This city can be very cruel to outsiders who have no idea about how fast the life is here," she says, voicing the emotions of most migrants who come here with hearts filled with desires, but have no idea about the struggle that awaits them.

"I was brought up in a family of engineers and it has been extremely difficult to convince them to let me pursue a career in modelling. I never succeeded in changing their minds and eventually I had to cut ties with them so I could achieve my dream. Blinded by my passion, I came to this city with very limited funds," says Karen. On the day she was to leave for Mumbai, Karen remembers her father's parting words: "Karen, I know you're leaving to do something that you think makes you happy. But please remember, that if it does not work out, I want you to do something else."

The past two years have been eventful for Karen: she has seen both sides of the so-called glamor industry—the good and the ugly. "There were days when I had only Rs 50 in my wallet and I had to survive on just that much the entire day. I learned to manage every single rupee I earned. Though unrelenting at first, my elder sister supported me and helped me financially," says Karen.

"During my early days in the modelling world I was cheated, exploited and insulted by casting agents. There were days when I had to go without food, since my financial resources were running dry. I travelled long distances all over the city, pleading with agencies to launch me and handing over my portfolio to anyone who seemed to be associated with the industry," Karen recalls.

She now lives in a rented flat in Malad and has her reasons for doing so. "Most struggling models and actors prefer living in the western suburbs, particularly Goregaon, Oshiwara, Lokhandwala,

Versova and Malad—the hubs of film studios. Living close to a studio ensures a certain level of access to the agencies."

But renting a house in these areas comes at a price. Quite a few struggling models get involved in either prostitution or gambling, dragging young men and women in the profession into disrepute. People in housing societies look down upon them and are usually hesitant about renting houses to single models. "They ask for details such as family photographs, proof of permanent residence, police verification, and documents from agencies where we are employed before renting us a flat," Karen reveals.

So far, Karen has done a few shoots in Mumbai for low-key brands and has worked for a few struggling makeup artists for their portfolios. However, that ultimate moment of glory hasn't come yet.

Like many others, Karen too has faced the ugly side of the industry. She recalls one horrifying incident at a party she attended with her colleagues. "When I started off as a model in the city, after a couple of meetings with casting agents, one of them began pursuing me and even made some really indecent proposals with the promise that he would help me 'make it big' in the city."

The only thing that has helped her survive two years in Mumbai is her attitude towards her work and her determination to not compromise herself and her values. It has taken her a long time to finally come to the conclusion that she will quit modelling and look for something else to do for a living.

"I have learned to channelise all my energies and frustration into finding a new passion for myself," Karen says proudly. Though ambitious, she is extremely realistic and smart. Not many possess the strength or wisdom to know when a dream is over and move on. Now 26, Karen has found her new calling: psychology. She is pursuing a degree via correspondence from Mumbai University.

Karen did not want to be a struggler all her life. "The modelling industry is all about making the right contacts and being at the right place at the right time. Most of the time in this world, dreams bite the dust and that makes people bitter. However, the key is to remain hopeful about a better future," says a now grown-up Karen.

"I have not failed. I have just found 10,000 things that do not work," she says, quoting Thomas Edison. She truly believes that success lies in constant hope and persistence, even in the face of disappointment.

Karen has not told her father about her change of profession and pleads anonymity. She plans to go back to her hometown after she gets her degree in psychology, apologise to her parents and mend broken ties.

"If there's one person I'd like to thank, it's my father. Had it not been for his words of wisdom long ago, I'd still be miserable and stuck in a never-ending nightmare. He has helped me understand that if Plan A doesn't work out, there is always Plan B," Karen says as she walks out with her copy of *The Social Animal* by Elliot Aronson.

Great depths

In the city of Mumbai, which runs at an overwhelmingly frantic pace, money is of utmost importance. In this race, managing to take care of yourself and your family is a task, let alone giving a thought to a stranger. Social networking is more important than getting to know the person sitting next to you. Rarely do we come across someone who makes a difference to people's lives. Those who do, often go unnoticed. This is the story of one such person who survives in a city that cares for no one.

Bunty Rao, a tall man, jauntily chats with his friends, sitting on the sidewalk near the entrance of Juhu beach, watching for clients with hawk eyes. With a Nikon DSLR camera around his neck and an album of sample photographs in his hand, he jumps to his feet any time someone steps onto the shore, offering to take their photographs against the backdrop of the gorgeous waves. Were it not for his T-shirt that says "Lifeguard on Duty", one would assume he is like any other photographer strolling on the beach. But Bunty is anything but ordinary.

Mumbai's beaches attract thousands of visitors every day, some from the city itself and others, tourists. Some come to gaze at the sea, some to eat and others to drench themselves in the warm, salty seawater. Alongside, hawkers throng the sand, selling balloons, peanuts, popcorn, bubbles, toys, robotic contraptions predicting the future and more.

"I've been working as a lifeguard with Baywatch Lifeguard Association (BLA) for 16 years," Bunty says, pointing to a board with the name of the NGO at the entrance. "It is probably one of the last things visitors will see or acknowledge. But this place would not be the same without that signboard."

Baywatch Lifeguard Association was established by Sayeed Shama, who realised that the security provided by BMC at beaches just wasn't enough to prevent accidents. He founded an NGO that trained men in civil defense. These men were positioned in different areas of the beach. Apart from the trained lifeguards, BLA also provides first-aid training and practical education on how to deal with emergencies to hawkers at the beach and regular visitors. "We don't charge a fee for our services. Everything we do is for free and for the people. We also clean the beach in the mornings," Bunty says. BLA believes in teaching people about civic responsibility and spreading awareness, expecting no monetary reward in return, just asking that civilians do their duty.

Bunty has been of great service to BLA. "I've saved around 50 lives in the 16 years I've worked here. One of the most dangerous times of the year is Ganesh *visarjan*. People go off into deep areas without caring about their safety," he says. There's a reason why Juhu beach is considered one of the safest in Mumbai. "I stay here till 10 pm every day to make sure things are okay. People call me in case of any emergency at the beach. There have been times when the beach is absolutely crowded and no one but me watches over the people. I've even featured in several newspaper articles," he reveals with a hint of pride.

Bunty wasn't always in Mumbai, though. He made this city his home over the years. "I came to Mumbai from Jamshedpur, Jharkhand, several years ago, leaving behind a job at SAP with the hope of earning a living. I always had a passion for photography and that passion was my saving grace in this city. Initially I dabbled with photography, till I landed the job of assisting in the making of a documentary. I also assisted in *Insaan* and *Bewafa*. Meanwhile, I pursued photography professionally by conducting photo-shoots at parties, weddings and corporate events. I even ventured into videography and making documentaries," he said. Naturally, the question of earning enough to survive in this city arises. Bunty earns Rs 500–600 per day, which sustains his family, who live in Madh Island.

That's Bunty Rao, who doesn't think twice before diving into the sea to rescue someone in danger. Respect sustains this unsung hero. His sense of responsibility drives him to make a difference every day. Bunty has never forgotten his dreams or his passions. He carries them forward and integrates them into his life the best he can. He is happy and content with his work and his life.

The tide begins to change as the sun goes down, the waters and the wind cool off, coconut trees sway in the early evening breeze. A whole new set of people flock to the beach as the others make their way home. The day draws to a close, but for Bunty, there's no stopping. He gets up from his seat, alert and energised, keeping vigil for anyone who might possibly need his help. He's the one the city needs; but he's the one who goes unnoticed.

Coolie no. 1035

It's just another day at Mumbai Central railway station. One of the busiest intercity junctions, a terminal for many long distance trains, it's always swarming with people. They come in taxis or cars full of luggage, all orchestrated by the shouts of competitive hawkers, the complaints of passengers about trains running late, lost newcomers asking for directions. In the midst of this din, resting on a luggage trolley, dressed in a faded red shirt, soiled white pants and a Nehru *topi*, 32-year-old Dattaram Avhad chats with his fellow porters. Their eight-hour shift has just ended, and this is break time.

"We belong to Sinnar, near Nasik. Being a family of farmers living in a drought prone area, we always faced financial difficulties. My father used to work as a coolie here in order to support us and also kept encouraging us to study," Dattaram says. Though a naughty child, Dattaram managed to study and completed his 12th grade in Arts. He also pursued a six-month course in electronics and computers, organised by the government. "Things weren't really working out well and studying further wasn't possible. Also, I couldn't find a decent job. So I decided to come to Mumbai."

With a few clothes and his father's coolie license, Dattaram came to Mumbai in 2001. He flashes his copper badge—a license porter tag provided by the railways for identification. "It can be passed down only through family. So either the son or a relative gets it when the coolie himself becomes unfit or too old to work," explains Dattaram. Are these badges up for sale? That one goes unanswered.

Interestingly, the term 'coolie' has etymological references in many Indian languages: *koli* in Gujarati, *kuli* in Tamil or *quli* in Urdu—all meaning daily wagers, manual labourers or slaves. It is also a historical term connected to the slave coolie trade that existed in colonial times. Coolies were used as cheap manpower in various labour intensive industries and also to work in mines and railway construction. In many parts of world, the word is considered a racial slur.

But in India the term has lingered on, in spite of the fact that it has been long since the coolies were transported across the country to help build the railways. Eventually they settled at these very railway stations to work as porters. Dattaram sits with his coolie friends, elaborating on his work life. "We have formed a labour union. This collective lets us fight for our rights and benefits. Like, for instance, we fought for permission to use the resting rooms. Initially we would have to pay 40 paisa, but today we pay Rs 1 for staying in the resting room." The union leader is usually a coolie chosen by a vote. "We work in shifts, while some work extra hours if they can." They plan their shifts so that they can take turns to rest and work.

In today's time of skyrocketing prices, Dattaram earns a meagre Rs 7,000, which he claims is sufficient to support his family. "We make the most of what we have here. We enjoy the India-Pakistan cricket matches by peeping into the waiting room. We also make sure that our senior coolies don't exert themselves, and take care of them. At the end of the day we pool all our money and then divide it equally, while also crediting those who have worked extra hours. Here we work and live as a family and help each other when anyone needs support, so that no one remains hungry." Dattaram wistfully adds how passengers will haggle even for Rs 10.

The union is also a means to negotiate with the railway authorities, which have not even included coolies as part of the official work force. "Coolies have been providing services to passengers and the railways for so long. We will be more than happy if we are accepted as a part of the railways," he grimly adds. Integration into the mainstream workforce is a continuing battle, especially given that states like Karnataka and Kerala have recognised coolies as Group D employees of the railways; they are also separately credited depending on their work and qualifications.

Dattaram works as a coolie for six months and spends the rest of the year with his family. Initially, like all other coolies, he used to wash his own clothes and depended on *dabbawallahs* for his meals. "When I went to Nashik in 2010, I got married and now I have a daughter. Recently, I took a small room on rent and now live with my family in Tardeo," he says. "I am working hard to educate my daughter. Also, perhaps one day, just like other families I meet here at the station, I too will take my family on a vacation!"

The duplicate

With so much unattainable in our city there is a demand for more accessible "duplicates"—whether it is a branded T-shirt or a Bollywood star. Navin Rathod sits in the lobby near the Gaiety cinema balcony doors. Under the electric blue lighting, Navin, with his uncanny likeness to Bollywood actor Anil Kapoor, fits in like an accenting element with the kitschy decor and film posters. Navin has been working as an usher at Gaiety for the last 25 years and has recently developed a parallel career as "Anil Kapoor".

Born in Mumbai on December 25, 1970, to parents from Bhavnagar, Gujarat, Navin was schooled in Mumbai. Even as he was growing up, people noticed his resemblance to Anil Kapoor. He was offered roles in ads and small modelling jobs, but refused, preferring to stay away from the camera. He took a job as an usher at the G7 mini-multiplex in Bandra.

"*Ramgarh ke Sholay* was the first film that I agreed to do, in 1990. The movie had an all-duplicate cast and was an eye-opening experience for me," says Navin. "Spending time in the company of other duplicates, like those of Shahrukh Khan and Amitabh

Bachchan, I began to understand the potential I held as the duplicate of a Bollywood star."

Since the release of his first film, Navin has had a steady flow of offers and work ranging from films to ads, stage events, reality shows and election campaigns. Even the original Anil Kapoor recommends him as a body double in his films. Navin feels lucky that unlike many other duplicates, he is blessed with Anil Kapoor's full support. They even co-starred in the film *No Entry*.

Navin takes being Anil Kapoor's duplicate very seriously. It goes beyond just being a doppelganger and extends to his clothing, gait, overall style and persona. He carries himself as Anil Kapoor would, and takes great pride in it, so much so that when Anil Kapoor complimented him, Navin's response was, "but of course my style is amazing, I am *your* duplicate, after all!"

When Navin performs live on stage, he is aware that the crowds come not to see Navin Rathod, but to experience Anil Kapoor's persona. When asked what the real Navin Rathod is like when he is not being Jr Anil Kapoor, he appears flummoxed. The Anil Kapoor persona is now hardwired into his own identity—Junior Anil Kapoor is who he is.

Apart from public recognition, one of the best parts of being Junior Anil Kapoor is the opportunities it has given him to travel and see the world. He has been to Dubai, Hong Kong, London, Los Angeles and New York for work, spending upto four months at a foreign location.

He has also travelled to Gujarat, Madhya Pradesh, Uttar Pradesh and around Maharashtra on election campaigns. He speaks in local accents, makes the crowd laugh and puts everyone in a good mood before the candidate speaks. It is quick and easy money.

In a city where copyright is not taken too seriously and all forms of duplicates are socially accepted, Navin Rathod has carved a niche for himself in the entertainment industry and his "original" is only flattered by it.

When requested for a photograph, Navin rushes to fetch his "goggles"—a pair of black Ray-Ban wayfarers (original or duplicate? One cannot help but wonder). He tucks in his shirt and proceeds to undo the buttons. He calls out to the theatre maintenance staff to switch on more lights in the lobby as he strikes a pose. Junior Anil Kapoor is ready for his shot.

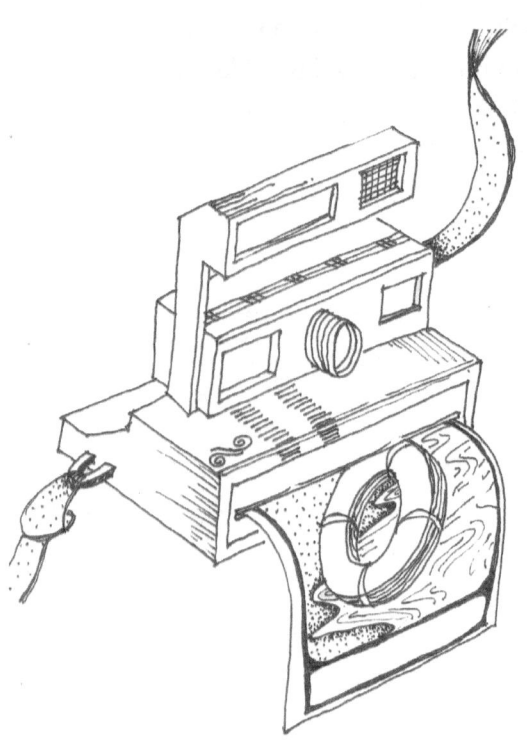

Khaala

In the story of our lives, more often than not we are the protagonists. Our point of view keeps us in the centre of things. Then there are those who live their lives around others. Growing up, I spent most of my time with Khaala, whose job it was to make me the centre of her story. She was my nanny, my housekeeper; she cooked for me and played with me. She left behind an identity as Safiya Ahmed Damad and lived with us like it was her own home. She was "Khaala", an Urdu term for aunt, but everyone called her that, irrespective of age. It took me 22 years to ask her who Safiya Ahmed Damad was, where she came from and how. After all these years, she is the protagonist of this story.

It begins with the search for gold. An ambitious man of the Habshi clan in Africa set out on a ship to the Konkan coast of India, with the promise of gold hidden in the sea shimmering in the depths of his eyes. He landed at Murud, a small fishing village with a beautiful beach. I ask Khaala if he found what he was searching for. "How else would he have become a Nawab?" she says. "Maybe that's why he loved the sea so much. He built the Janjira fort so he could live surrounded by crashing waves." Legend has it that the Habshi Nawab sacrificed his son's life to build the fort.

"They struggled to build it; the walls wouldn't stand, no matter how much mortar he used. Then one night the Nawab had a dream. He dug a pit and dropped his ring in it and asked his son to retrieve it. As soon as the boy jumped in, he ordered the pit to be filled with mud. Some people will give up anything for the sake of ambition."

Safiya is a descendent of this clan. Her childhood was spent playing within the fort walls, where the Habshis lived until the 1990s. Janjira has a reputation for being impregnable and was unconquered until the government of India relocated its residents to a nearby village called Rajpur. Safiya's father worked in the Nawab's house. He was gifted a house that was entirely inherited by her brother, since women had no right to inheritance. He now runs a hotel in the house by the beach. Safiya was given in marriage to the Damad family living in the house across. Her husband sold his share of property in Murud and decided to move to Mumbai, where he bought a flat in BPT Colony, Wadala, and worked as an instructor in Janjira Motor School, Bhindi Bazaar. Here, Safiya started her own family. When she was 30, however, her husband passed away, with four daughters and a son to support.

Safiya's education had ended when she was in class two, for the sake of her brother's studies. She now had to begin the process of searching for a way to bring up her children alone. During this time she did several odd jobs—delivering buckets of water to people's homes where municipality lines hadn't yet reached, sewing buttons on shirts, making *papad* for Lijjat—anything to put food on her children's plates.

Her building watchman, who was also Konkani, got her a job

in the packaging department of a fish exporting company. Being from a fishing village, she used her innate knowledge to classify fish by breed. "There were many workers for packaging, but only three Konkanis were chosen to classify fish," she says, with a tinge of pride.

In 1984 she left Wadala. "There was a man in our building, a goon...everyone was scared of him. Sometimes he would enter our house, drunk, in the dead of the night. I had four young girls; I was scared for their safety," Safiya tells me. So she packed her things and shifted base to Mumbra, a quiet, clean, mostly forested suburb which became a Muslim ghetto after the 1991–1992 riots. The unorganised, haphazard urbanisation of Mumbra, once green with mangroves, can be attributed to the ease with which one can acquire a flat here, without the hassle of official paperwork. The building industry is run mostly illegally, contributing to the urban sprawl.

Named after Mumbra Devi, a Koli and Agri deity whose temple adorns one of the surrounding peaks, Mumbra has now become one of the fastest growing Muslim ghettos in the city. Amenities are low and employment opportunities limited, but Mumbra is a hub for immigrant Muslims searching for a safe abode with community support.

Safiya's children have all chosen to settle here. Her granddaughters sit around her as she tells me her story. They are still studying, but have reached marriageable age, as the trend in the community goes. One of the girls is studying for her chartered accountancy entrance test, Safiya tells me, her chest swelling with pride. The place of women in her community may still be low, but Safiya is equally respected by them all. Her determination and enterprising nature enabled her to achieve what seemed impossible. She survived, and so did her children. She is their mother and their godmother. She is

"Safiya", Arabic for "pure", her skin smooth and unwrinkled, even at 67. But for me, she will remain my Khaala, who brought me up and taught me to love fish curry, adding to my roots a sliver of her Konkan, her homeland.

The land of the *vadapav*

"Bara Handi in Byculla is one of the lesser known food revelations in the city. Come Ramadan, the place is chock-a-block with stalls selling *paya* (goat's trotter soup) and kebabs, and the aroma wafting through the gullies signals the coming alive of this section of the city at night," says Kalyan Karmakar, market researcher by day and food blogger by night. There are very few people in the city who know as much about Mumbai's food culture as him, and fewer still who could have managed to spin a profession out of an enthusiasm for food. Kalyan pioneered the concept of paid food walks around the city—he guides groups of people to a selection of good eateries in the city to sample the food and get a true taste of the city. He has written articles for publications such as *Femina* and *Hindustan* Times. "Finely Chopped", his food blog, has been hugely popular since its inception seven years ago.

For Kalyan the city is divided into stretches belonging to a particular communities and their food. It is a lens through which to look at the city, to understand its intricacies by tracking the subtle changes in the food scene over the years. With the influx of molecular gastronomy and world cuisines, the local cuisines embedded in the fabric of the city are diminishing. The Irani cafés, with their "Do not tip the waiter" signs, marble-top tables and glass cases filled with baked treats have all but shut down. No longer does one find intellectuals mulling over coffee and a book in buzzing spaces; they are being replaced by expensive coffee shops and fast food joints. The Maharashtrian belt of Parel and Dadar, with its kiosks selling *varan bhaat* and *jhunka bhakar*, feeds hundreds of hungry commuters, placing them at opposite end of the spectrum from swanky places in Bandra and Khar.

All these insights find mention in Kalyan's writing. "I was transferred to Mumbai from Kolkata in 2009. I spent my weekends exploring the city and scouring food joints. Initially my friends used to take me around, but I developed a taste for the city by discovering it bit by bit through food," he says.

He cannot help but compare the foods of Kolkata and Mumbai: Kolkata, despite being a city of gastronomic delights, fades in comparison with Mumbai. "Though the people are far more passionate about food, there is not much in terms of the variety available there. Here, there is a truly cosmopolitan outlook when it comes to food. I can sample Keralite and Mangalorean delicacies as well as rare Parsi food." This trait can be traced back to Mumbai's ethnic diversity, with a variety of communities bringing their own set of dishes to the metaphorical table. The Parsis brought in the Irani cafés, there are homestays offering Konkan food near Versova, the Bandra Chapel Road stretch offers the choicest *marzipans* around Christmas. These become markers in history. The Goan history of Grant Road is remembered in terms of the aroma of *xacuti* and *sorpotel* wafting out through open kitchen windows, spilling onto the streets below.

The migrant coming into the city does not do so with a clean slate, but brings along his own set of dogmas. Kalyan's case was no different. Fresh out of the land of *maacher jhol* (fish curry) and rice, he entered a Maharashtrian restaurant to encounter something completely alien. "I saw people eating fish with *roti*. In West Bengal that would have been blasphemy. Fish is meant to be eaten with rice, such that its delicate nature is not masked by the strong flavours of the *roti*." After many such instances, he now encounters food with no such preconceived notions. The idea is to experience everything as it comes, and save judgement for later.

A few years earlier, it would have been unthinkable to have a career in food outside of hotel management. But today, food walks and blogs, food photography, or specialising in only a certain number of dishes have become valid and lucrative careers. Not to mention the immense satisfaction of pursuing a passion unhindered by financial woes. Kalyan's food walks are his only source of income at the moment as he finishes writing his book on his food experiences, 'The Travelling Belly'. Other companies such as Petpujari and Mumbai Travelogue also sponsor paid food walks in Mumbai, mostly catering to expats and a few local aficionados. Kalyan discovers, rediscovers and explores his city with a bunch of likeminded people, through his favourite lens: food. As he presides over a group enjoying food that could disappear in a few years, he has the satisfaction of knowing that he, in his own way, has contributed to conserving a part of Mumbai's cultural heritage in collective memory.

Master of a few arts

Across Mahatma Gandhi Road, opposite the ogive-arches of the David Sassoon Library, Elphinstone College and the Department of Archives is a fenced sidewalk outlining the plot of the art precinct of Mumbai in the Old Fort area. The area is home to Jehangir Art Gallery, the Prince of Wales Museum and Max Mueller Bhavan. The pavement is a quasi-gallery for downtown Mumbai's poorer artists to display their *chef d'oeuvres* to pedestrians, and for smatterings of art conversation that usually can't take place within the sanctimonious cavities of art galleries, where silence and hushed critique are the rules of the game.

As you walk from under the Jehangir Art Gallery's curved entrance canopy to the Museum's main gate, you meet the stalwart of the group: old, wise, mellow, melancholic, world-weary and bearded, Mr Gani.

"My father came here from Gulbarga in Karnataka in 1952, when I was eight. He was a textile artist, steeped in the art of Qalamkari. This art form goes back generations in my family; we were almost a guild. When he came here he didn't find much work for his textiles, so he did miscellaneous work, always ready to do creative handiwork, painting, textile design, teaching art. It was a hereditary trait," says Gani. His hometown, which had once flourished under the influence of the Golconda Sultanate, was the centre for Qalamkari artists during the trade boom of the 16th century.

Qalamkari, or "pen craftsmanship" in Persian, is the old art-science of fabric painting on chintz or calico, an ancient, familial enterprise in central India that has been bastardised into an urban enterprise of mass textile design using block-printing methods that have made it less complicated than it was a few centuries ago. "The 17-step practice—it takes that many even in the 21st century—requires careful penmanship to make the blocks, using a *qalam* and black dye to draw an outline of the design—traditional motifs that are extremely intricate. And in that practice of free-flowing lines, a certain respect is retained," explains Gani.

"If you look at the big picture, we're all originally Iranians, filtering through the Kutch to the Deccan. Dad's two brothers and he lived together in a few huts in Gulbarga in absolute squalor. He took the train to Mumbai after the birth of his fourth child, my sister. He told me that he was fed up of living in that camel town," Gani remembers. "He eventually became an interior decorator in Khadi Bazaar. My mother remained a textile artist, doing odd jobs in the new textile companies that were popping up all over the Fort area. This remained with me—my parents' willingness to do anything for and with art."

Gani studied at the JJ School of Arts. "And once I got into the rhythm of creating art for bread, after I graduated, I lost the carefreeness of my school days. When I was 14, I used to sit in a theatre balcony every day for 12 hours, watching foreign movies:

Ben-Hur, Helen of Troy, McKenna's Gold...you know, those old westerns, movies that had a slow pace. I think I've watched 7,000 movies, and I'm not kidding," reminisces Gani. "I played tons of domestic cricket too in those Mumbai leagues: Harris Shield, Giles Shield, Kanga League. I got Gavaskar out once too. Cricket was something every boy tried out then, and I found out I was a good fast bowler."

Soon he began working as an art teacher in municipal schools at Dongri and Nagpada schools and stayed there for 40 years. "Students were doing nothing much all day besides watching teachers write symbols on boards and copying them. So when the bell for my art class rang, it meant they were finally allowed to make their *own* symbols. Recently, I bumped into one of them; he was participating in an Indo-Japanese program near by. He here bumped into me, recognised me at second glance and then poured out his heart about his life since those green days. Kids these days have so many more opportunities."

Coming back to his art practice, Gani says, "I made most of my commercial paintings in my *makaan* studio in Pydhonie, attached to my house; it's not a huge space, but it gets the job done. I got them displayed at Jehangir when I was younger, but my most recent tryst with the gallery in 2009 ended in a big loss. I guess interests have risen and I am now just small fry. But yeah, I was quite famous then, getting displayed in Europe too, though I've never been there."

A motley collection of Rs 1,000-a-piece watercolour paintings on one foot by one foot squares of paper sit inside plastic bags to save them from the rain, adorning the fence behind him. Most depict bucolic settings: pastures, meadows and forests. And others are marine: a lighthouse, a ship in a tempest, a beach. They are in sharp contrast to the surroundings: swarms of cacophonous people, dogs and vehicles bustling through the evening melee. "*Where earth, air and water meet, oh joy fills my soul,*" Gani quotes an Urdu verse.

"Going back to the roots—that's where it begins and ends. This agglutinated city cannot sustain my soul; my soul has to be replenished by connecting with nature. Especially since I live here, in downtown Mumbai, I yearn to go out into the countryside. It's all about finding my tranquil place. That's where I make my art: on a beach or in a ruined temple far from the obfuscating shoulders of these concrete buildings. I've travelled all over India—the Himalayas, Hampi, Kanyakumari, Benaras, everywhere—and I've captured all those places on paper," says Gani.

"I don't make much money, but a conversation like this makes up for the tedium. Discussing being a cog in the wheel of Mumbai is good for an old cog like me. Sometimes I wonder what would have happened if I had moved away from my society, if I had broken convention and travelled abroad to make a name for myself. But it's my choice and no one can take that from me."

Many fractions, one community

Mangaldas Market is one of the biggest and oldest wholesale clothes bazaars in Mumbai, tucked away in the bylanes of Bhuleshwar. A walk through it is like a dream for fabric lovers, who could get lost in the vast variety of colourful and vibrant ethnic-wear, Indian textiles, bales of imported material and much more. In a dingy lane of the labyrinth is the low-profile Dwarkesh Creations, a textile shop set up in 1989, that captures the spirit of the city's enterprising Gujarati community.

Dwarkesh Creations is co-owned by the Shah Brothers—Atul and Chandresh. "My father, Gopaldas Mathuradas Shah, came to Mumbai post-Independence in 1958. He was a man of high aims. He couldn't imagine staying in the small village of Vadnagar, Gujarat, owning a small shop or doing anything, for that matter," says Atul Gopaldas Shah.

Gopaldas Shah arrived in Mumbai with Rs 150 in his pockets and a dream of a good life, something he sensed his village couldn't provide. In Mumbai, he stayed in a *chawl* with his elder brother and decided to try his hand at the *kapda* bazaar near Crawford market. The market was established in 1893, predominantly by Gujarati traders. Its nine narrowly divided lanes house over 200 shops. The market has 19 entrances, which increase the chances of getting lost.

"My father began as a broker in the *kapda* market, earning Rs 100 per month. He used to send half his income to his parents and save as much as possible from the rest so as to invest in the future. He had a very good sense for business," the younger brother, Chandresh says, beaming with pride.

Gopaldas made many contacts and associates in Mumbai and the market, being dominated by a Gujarati community, worked to his benefit. In a short time he mastered the art of trading and amassed a small fortune.

In 1963 he went back to his village and married Kapilaben Shah. In the initial years Kapilaben stayed with her in-laws in the village and Gopaldas travelled there once in three months to meet his family. "When travelling back by train my father would wear a pair of pants and carry one pajama with him; once the journey commenced, he would swap those so that the pants didn't get dirty. He would rarely splurge on himself," says Atul.

The shop was named Dwarkesh Creations out of religious sentiment. Names like Srinathji, Balaji and Krishna are commonly used by traders in the Gujarati community. The tiny shops in the market are built on raised platforms and the owners sit comfortably on mattresses.

Soon Kapilaben returned to Mumbai with her husband and they rented a 10-square-foot room in a *chawl* in Jogeshwari, located beside a *tabela*. The strong stench made Kapilaben ill in the first month of their stay. So after pooling in enough resources Gopaldas and his elder brother and family shifted to Kandivali, where they bought a flat in the Kailash Nagar Cooperative Housing Society.

A year after their marriage the couple was blessed with their first child, Atul, and four years later their second son, Chandresh was born. "He provided us with good education opportunities and encouraged us to become independent and taught us to earn a good living for ourselves. He made us well aware of the importance of money and savings. The values that he inculcated in us have been very helpful," says Atul.

The elder son joined his father in 1990 and got all the necessary business training from a close associate, Vijay. "Vijaybhai and we invested money and started a business in partnership of exporting cloth," the elder son recalls. After a few years Vijay left the business and the younger son joined; the business continued to grow and prosper.

"During the initial days we would get our raw materials from South India, but later, as the nature of the markets changed, we started getting materials from Panipat," explains Chandresh Shah. Impressed with his son's business practices, Gopaldas handed over the shop to the brothers and continued his job as a broker on a smaller scale. Over the years the firm has expanded to three times its original size.

"My father was a very principled and hardworking man his whole life; he passed away in 2010," states his younger son. In 2008, the brothers decided to branch out into the wholesale market and started a new office in Kandivali, near their residence.

The Shahs lived as a joint family with Gopaldas, his wife and their sons, and their son's wives and children. They continue to be very close today.

The third generation of the family is pursuing careers in different fields, none of them interested in joining the family business. This doesn't perturb the two brothers: "Both of us strongly believe in allowing our children to follow their own dreams, just like our father allowed us," says Atul with a smile, looking at his brother, who gives an approving nod.

The brothers feel that the Gujarati community has made very important contributions to the country's economy and Bhuleshwar is the biggest hub of Gujarati traders hawking cloth, steelware and jewellery.

Mangaldas Market, while being just one part of Mumbai's chaotic market maze, is fascinating. It shows how these shops are a very small fraction of the larger trading community that has settled here over the years and changed the economic image of the city. Vendors, owners and buyers jostle through the overcrowded lanes as they live, trade and coexist.

The boy called theatre

The Prithvi Theatre's surroundings are illuminated by lights hanging from the branches of a large tree in the café; colourful streamers brighten up the space. The café is abuzz with incessant chatter. This is where students whiling away their time and theatre aficionados meet. There's never a lack of energy and enthusiasm: there is something about Prithvi that stirs up excitement and discussion. Past the café, behind the bookstore and the entrance to the theatre, in a space for performers there is another buzz reaching a crescendo. Atul Kumar is chatting with the members of his crew. His show, "Noises Off" is to start in two hours. Several rehearsals have been done, improvisations made, and it is time to perform. The crew is more than welcoming. They laugh and relax with cups of tea, *chaat* and a cigarette or two.

"I've always been interested in theatre, but I've never been able to work for anyone. I always wanted to start something of my own, so I started my own theatre company," Atul says casually. The Company Theatre has produced plays like *The Blue Mug, Numbers in the Dark, Noises Off, Lady with Lapdog, Rosencrantz & Guildenstern are Dead,*

The Chairs, Richard III, Voices, Smell, Hair and many others. The company has organised theatre related seminars, conferences, and workshops for all age groups, besides performances, collaborations and interactions with other forms of art and performance.

"It has been quite a ride since I moved to Mumbai in 1997. I met all kinds of people when I came here. Back then, I befriended Sanjana Kapoor, who gave me Prithvi to work in. (Sanjana ran Prithvi Theatre from 1993 to 2012.) She never let me feel insecure and has been there for me in all my endeavours," he says.

Prithvi Theatre was founded in 1942 by Prithviraj Kapoor, whose dream was to have a permanent place for his theatre company. It was eventually built as a *pucca* structure in 1978. It fostered the healthy growth of theatre with all its experimentation and variety and continues to be a space exploding with new ideas. Its doors are always open for new performers and companies. It welcomes anything that pushes the existing rules and boundaries of theatre beyond the limit, while keeping audiences flooding in at the same time.

"One of the first things I noticed when I came to Mumbai was how beautiful, free and bohemian it was. I find Mumbai a really sexy city. I find the sea sexy, the monsoon is sexy. This city introduced me to a lot of people. It has been a fantastic experience," Atul muses. Being open to art and other creative endeavours, Mumbai was the right place for Atul to be in.

It is cumbersome to set up a studio in the city dedicated to the production and rehearsal of plays because of the astronomical real estate prices. He believes that theatre needs that kind of space to grow. So he started a residency in Kamshet called the Company Theatre Workspace, which is another manifestation of his passion for theatre.

"We started the residency at Kamshet in March two years ago. It has been my dream for a long time. It is a "laboratory" out of the city where we can work without distractions. It is a space for theatre companies to rehearse and create freely. We've made three productions in two years. We're creating a new kind of work.

"It hasn't taken off as much as I'd want it to, yet, but it's happening. It wasn't an easy process. A lot of effort was put into buying the land and creating this workspace. It has an environment for concentrated and relaxed laboratory work in performance art and theatre, which is what I've always wanted," explains Atul.

"We've produced plays of all genres. We've conducted workshops for all age groups and have travelled all over the country and to places across the globe with our work. It has been a long journey since The Theatre Company was founded in 1993. Of course we try to experiment as much as possible. Given a choice I'd experiment more, but we have to keep preferences of the audience in mind. So we have to find a balance between the kind of work we want to create and what the audience would want to see," he says.

Atul explains, "Often theatre comes across as something exclusively for the intelligentsia and the elite; however, Prithvi tries to make it accessible to everybody. It isn't always successful in changing perceptions, but audiences do spill over from existing Marathi and Gujarati shows. So theatre has always had an audience in Mumbai. People are beginning to show a keen interest in theatre and its development. Getting a good audience is as big a challenge as making good plays. As artistes, we naturally want to try and create new work that people of the city haven't experienced before. Unlike Bollywood, theatre needs to struggle more to keep people coming in for shows. The struggle is not only for space to make more interesting work, but also to draw people into their vision. Theatre as a field of art has potential, but faces many challenges. It has been a beautiful experience and I have no regrets whatsoever," Atul smiles. Atul Kumar is now well known in the realms of both theatre and Bollywood. His talent and vision are respected and praised.

The buzz in the café is increasing. Backstage, next to the green rooms, Sachin Kamani (who makes shows happen and markets them) is conducting a sound check for the play. The green rooms are small, plush and bohemian, like the people of Prithvi. The images on the walls, the colours and the décor add warmth to the place, enhanced by the close-knit family of theatre artists. One actor is rehearsing in a room. Another reads a script. On the stage, Sujay Saple (actor) helps Sachin adjust the sound. People are already in their seats.

An hour later, *Noises Off* begins. The comedy unwraps smoothly, with a well written script and seamless acting. Atul's rigour and need for freedom in his work is reflected in his plays. He has a liking for Shakespeare and constantly reinvents his plays with his vision and taste. Twenty minutes into the play, Atul enters and watches his dream play out before his eyes.

The vibrance of theatre in the city is as apparent as its need for space for its healthy growth. There are new plays every week by different theatre companies. Theatre and other forms of art are flourishing in centres like Prithvi, which give them a home. Online platforms help with advertising and arouse interest. Theatre, however, needs space to encourage experimentation. In his own way Atul Kumar has nurtured a space and a platform to create work undisturbed, thereby playing his part in the larger interests of theatre in the city and the rest of the world.

Next station: Nallasopara

It's just another Monday morning and the railway platform is crowded, as usual. Impatient passengers crib about trains running late in between sips of coffee and breakfast. People seem eager to jump into the train before it stops, to secure a seat. But life becomes relatively easy when someone clambers in early and reserves space for his train friends, or, in local train language, his "group". Ronnie Lobo is one such lucky person who belongs to a group. "My train journeys are fun, and my only worry is to enter the train from Nallasopara. My group consists of people from Vasai, Nallasopara and Virar. We enter at Nallasopara and reserve seats for our colleagues who will be entering at Virar." The journey from Nallasopara to Virar and back takes 10 minutes, and the waiting period at Virar is another 20 minutes. In the process, they lose about 30 minutes of extra journey time just to secure a seat.

Once settled in, the one-and-a-half-hour journey is enjoyed by the group—they take turns to sit. The members joke or discuss current affairs. Some groups sing *bhajans* or try their best at rendering hit Hindi film melodies of the 1970s and the 1980s.

"My great–grandfather, who was originally from Goa, was working in Karachi and my grandfather later came to Bombay and started working at Cox & Kings and then started staying in a rented place in Marine Lines," says Ronnie.

Before Independence the two ports on the West coast of undivided India were Bombay and Karachi. Goa was a Portuguese colony from the early 1500s to 1961, so natives of Goa would go to Bombay, Karachi or Africa in search of work on board the ships.

"My father too stayed on a rental basis in Byculla and later took a flat on leave and license basis at Colaba. He initially worked for Thomas Cook and thereafter for Mercantile Bank, which was renamed Hongkong & Shanghai Banking Corporation. Meanwhile, my grandfather built a bungalow in Goa that cost him Rs 5,000, which was a big amount in the late 1930s!"

Between the 1920s and the 1950s rooms were available on rent quite easily, perhaps because Bombay wasn't as densely populated as it is today. In 1961 Ronnie's parents found a flat in Colaba, a prime location.

"As a kid, when I was around 10 years old, I recall watching fireballs in the sky that were fired by the Indian Navy ships from Bombay Harbour, as there was a rumour of Pakistani air attacks. The radios and newspapers were used to create awareness about the tension that existed then. We would stick brown paper on glass panels so as to not let the light out and at times we were warned with sirens during high alert to switch off all the lights off. This was during the Indo-Pak war in December 1971."

Some evenings would be spent at the Gateway of India or in the park of the Prince of Wales Museum or at the Bandstand garden adjacent to the Cooperage ground, watching children ride past on horseback. Ronnie remembers the panoramic view from the fifth floor balcony, with the Express Towers and the Air India building on one side and the neon advertisement of Finlays on top of Churchgate station in front; on the other side was the Rajabai clock tower, from where his father would set the time on his watch, and which was later blocked by the New India Assurance Building. And towards the right side of their balcony they could view ships at the Bombay harbour and the village of Uran across the water.

"In 1973 the Bombay Rent Act was amended and licensees were given the status of protected tenants. Nevertheless, my parents voluntarily handed over the keys of the flat to the owner in 1974 without taking a single paisa and purchased a home at Vile Parle West." The impact of the amendment to the Bombay Rent Act in 1973 left many owners at the mercy of their protected tenants.

In 1989 Ronnie booked a flat at Nallasopara and moved into it in 1992, by which time he was married. "While living in Colaba I was in the heart of the city. When I moved to Vile Parle West, I thought I had come too far, but now, staying at Nallasopara, I realise how close Vile Parle was to South Mumbai!"

This conversation takes place on the evening train. As Ronnie winds up his conversation about his own journey, sitting amongst passengers eager to reach the warmth of their homes after a hard day's work, one can hear the automated announcement: "next station: Nallasopara".

Of bats, balls and bets

While most people get done with work by the evening, several people get ready to leave for their night shifts. Not all, however, have legitimate businesses to get to. At 11 pm, one of the rooms in Sunil Fifadra's (name changed) five-bedroom flat in the suburb of Malad is ready for business. With five or more mobile phones constantly ringing, computers placed around his bed and the television switched on to the sports channel, Sunil, a plump man of 46, gets ready for the cricket match scheduled to begin soon. Constantly checking for updates on his phone he says in Gujarati, "I came to Mumbai to educate myself and to graduate. I never had intentions to do wrong things and according to me, betting on cricket matches just happened as a matter of chance."

In a small town called Khambhat in Gujarat, Fifadra grew up playing cricket in his ancestral home with neighbours and friends. "My father got a government job in Mumbai in the 1970s or something and brought me here. In those days, getting a government job was a matter of pride and honour. But I just wanted to become somebody really big," says Sunil, his attention now off his phones.

"I finished my graduation in Commerce and started working at a small office in the diamond market. My initial income was Rs 200 a month, pretty good for a beginner then, but I wanted faster money."

Sunil started punting on small cricket matches in and around Malad, the colony he stayed in. "In those days, the only bets I could lay were on the games that were played in the *chawl* compound by the local people. It was only after we got radios and popular media that betting on international cricket matches became possible. We would assemble at a friend's place and lay our bet; TV sets were a luxury. For every match we would win, I would treat my parents to a movie and popcorn. Today, times have changed from radios and televisions to computers and mobile phones. They are a boon as well as a big curse. I have shifted to an apartment from the *chawl* I lived in. This apartment is where I work, eat and pray."

Sunil married soon after he graduated and has two children who have completed their schooling. "I wanted to give my children all the luxuries—that is primarily why I continued to lay bets and eventually became a bookie. My children love me for who I am. My wife supports me in the work I do and has faith in my morals. She doesn't like the fact that I use our bedroom as my workplace, because she has to sleep in another room, alone at times. But she understands. Today I have cars, houses, educated children and a loving wife. I feel my life is the happiest."

Talking about how his work life has changed, Sunil says, "The advent of technology has given us a global market to make deals. With websites like Bet-fair it has become safe to engage with a global business market that is legal in other countries. New weather applications also give us a fairer judgement of how the game will turn out. Unfortunately, more accessibility also increases risk, because phones, IP addresses, etc., can be tapped by other devices."

Punting and laying bets on cricket and other forms of sports are considered illegal under the Indian Penal Code. Sunil, nicknamed "Slysha" by his peers, says that everyone in the market has a nickname to give a false impression to the police and maintain secrecy. About the law-and-order scene in the city he says, "It becomes nasty when you have to deal with cops. During IPL matches and World Cups we shift our base to Goa or Lonavala, at our farmhouses, to protect so that our names and numbers. The Mumbai police have got better with their jobs; we don't blame them, but it isn't our fault either. Even they get their cut; we bribe them and they have to stay put. It works both ways. Nobody is a man of God."

He describes the turmoil in the profession: "There are times when there are back-to-back matches and you have to be awake all night, because 20-20s are real cliff-hangers. Sometimes you are under tremendous pressure because you have laid heavy bets, and sometimes you lose. Staying consistent is difficult. Often we get threats from people; many times people refuse to pay up when they lose. It adds a lot of tension, but it is all part of the game. I am like a batsman—sometimes I hit a century, sometimes I get bowled out with the first ball. But I have learned some sportsman spirit at least," he laughs.

Sunil points out that it is interesting to see the level of acceptance modern Mumbai society has shown. He says that however broad-minded we think we have become, we are still the same, trying to live in a world shunned for being what it is.

"Who is not corrupt? The major problem is the social stigma that is attached to the profession, along with the police atrocities. If it is okay to punt in casinos, try your luck with lottery tickets and bet on who will become the prime minister of India, then this seems fairly justified. The system we live in is corrupt, shallow and dodgy. We are all hypocrites trying to show ourselves as ideal citizens to the world," insists Sunil. "Most people have an issue with the kind of work I do, with the kind of businesses and people I deal with, but that does not affect me, because somewhere I know my ideals are intact." Increasing the television volume and shifting his gaze towards the game, he starts dialling a number to make his next bet.

A universal escape strategy

The capoeirista has
the coordination of a dancer,
the flexibility of a gymnast,
the strength of a martial artist,
the endurance of a marathon runner,
the beat of a drummer
and the heart of a philosopher.

Today, people flock to martial arts classes for various reasons—some want to stay fit, some want to learn self-defence and others are looking for a way to counter the stress of urban living.

In a nondescript lane in Khar is a studio space, the first Indian centre of Capoeira Cordao de Ouro headed by Instructor Baba, an energetic, charismatic 40-something man with fitness and flexibility levels that belie his age. His enthusiasm and energy transcend the Bandra studio and infect every student in his class. The group of about 30 students is bubbling with excitement. Practising a non-violent, escape-oriented means of self-defence, Capoeiristas move agilely to the beat of drums and the tune of a traditional slave song sung in Portuguese by those standing around. The rhythmic clapping and cheering resonate through the room; the euphoria is palpable. With all its excitement and energy, the session looks more like a dance routine than a fight. They call it "playing Capoeira".

With its non-violent philosophy, social nature, music and dance-like movements, Capoeira, which originated in Brazil, fits the Indian ethos, though it was introduced to the country only in 2006 by Reza Baba Massah, a Capoeirista who learned the art form in Israel. He is known simply as "Baba" in Capoeira circles.

Reza was born in India to parents from Iran and Iraq. Soon after, the family left India and settled in Iran. The Revolution of 1979 forced them to leave Iran and move back to India. Reza studied at the Barnes Boarding school in Deolali. In 1988 his family moved out of India again, this time to Israel.

Speaking to a new batch of students Baba says, "Capoeira has made me what I am. It has become a way of life for me." They listen attentively. "I initially wanted to be a pilot and went to Australia to train. I travelled to Canada to complete the required flying hours and that was where I first watched Capoeira. There were a few Christian missionaries standing on the street holding placards about Jesus and next to them was a group of men of African origin, doing back-flips, kicks, ducks and handstands in a seemingly coordinated way, with others beating drums and singing around them. I did not know about Capoeira at the time and thought to myself, 'What on earth are these men doing?' But my interest had been aroused. The men exuded a positive energy that drew me and I was fascinated by their vibrancy, moves and flexibility. I could not get it out of my head for a long time!"

Baba was hooked. "I returned to Israel, where finding a pilot's job was slow progress, so I decided to open a café, since my other passion was cooking. I set up a café in a mall, but as luck would have it, on the day of the opening there was a bomb blast in the city. People were scared and stayed at home and the mall was deserted. No friends or family turned up for the opening. There was one area in the mall, however, which was buzzing with activity—a fitness studio near my café. Hearing music, clapping and cheering, I peered through the blinds and saw the room packed with people playing Capoeira, unfazed by the bombs. There was a high level of energy and a cheerful vibe in the room. I thought, "If these people are here for their class even today, they would make ideal patrons for my new café!" In my attempt to befriend them, I struck a deal with the head instructor of the class, Mestre Cueca. It was decided that I would join his Capoeira class and he, in turn, would eat at my café regularly. I started attending the class and before I knew it, I was hooked." It was Mestre Cueca who named him Baba and in turn, Baba gives each of his students a Capoeira name.

Baba met his wife on a visit to Bombay. He was on his way to Sterling cinema for a movie and lost his way. A young lady helped him with directions, they became friends, fell in love and got married. She moved to Israel to live with him. It was her idea to bring Capoeira to India. Speaking to her friends in Mumbai, she realised that no one in the city knew about it. A Google search on Capoeira India found just one result: Akshay Kumar had listed it as one of the seven deadliest martial arts. Today the same search leads to five pages of results about Baba's training centres and his students!

Baba and his wife saw potential in India for Capoeira training and also hoped to open a restaurant in Mumbai. They moved to the city in 2005. Once again the restaurant did not work out, but in 2006 Baba set up a Capoeira centre in Bandra and started teaching. His first class had four students.

For the next four years, Baba taught adults. The number of students grew steadily; people were drawn to the art form because of its universal appeal and philosophy. Just as the slaves had used Capoeira to alleviate trauma, people turn to Capoeira today to help deal with their urban frustration and stress. While training, they are able to shut out the problems of the outside world, and they leave the class feeling rejuvenated and alive.

Capoeira developed as an underground art form in Brazil, created by African slaves who needed a way to deal with the repression of slavery. It emphasised escape moves and gave its practitioners hope. In Israel, drawn by its universal appeal, Muslims and Jews play Capoeira together and relish the sense of community formed within the group. In Mumbai, many students in Baba's group are young professionals who have migrated to the city from elsewhere. Through Capoeira, strong bonds are formed between these individuals and they become a family of sorts, supporting one another in a new environment.

"Training just adults was not very profitable, since several of my students are broke. But after watching my own son take to Capoeira, I started teaching children as well and soon found it very rewarding. Since children are more flexible, they are able to learn quicker and there are many more takers in the younger age groups. Capoeira is both practical and relevant today, with all the bullying and child molestation. It is i workout for the entire body and combined with its non-violent philosophy, it makes a good alternative to regular

PE sessions in schools," Baba explains. He clarifies that Capoeira teaches children not to pick a fight, but how to get out of one. Several Mumbai schools have already included Baba's Capoeira programme as part of their curriculum.

Baba and his group also work with many Mumbai-based NGOs, conducting workshops for children from Dharavi, the Khar slum and orphanages and children of sex workers. These underprivileged kids are the most receptive and eager to learn. Baba and his troupe are examples of how Capoeira can change life—they give hope to these children, a means of escape from their disadvantaged lives, while having fun with an activity that challenges physical abilities. Where college graduates are hesitant, these children, with fewer opportunities, might take their knowledge of Capoeira to another level by becoming instructors themselves, Baba hopes.

Several of Baba's adult students have already started teaching the martial art form; a young MBA graduate and an engineer are just two of the students who have chosen it as a full time job. It has become more than just a hobby; it is now a way of life for them, which they find more satisfying than any desk job.

As awareness of Capoeira grows in the city, more people are including it in their fitness regimen, with Baba's students-turned-instructors teaching even Bollywood personalities—Aamir Khan, for instance, learned the form for his film *Dhoom 3*. Cordao de Ouro now has 16 centres around the city and has even spread its arms to Bangalore and Goa.

Spreading a smile, telling stories through movement and song, Capoeira is, Baba says, "like food—it feeds you with vibrations, energy and joy".

The Cordao de Ouro group does shows along Carter Road in Bandra, beating drums, strumming *berimbaus*, clapping and singing, while pairs take turns to play Capoeira in the centre of the circle. They will always draw a curious audience, people who are more than happy to join in the fun.

Torrents of reel

Getting off the escalator on the top floor of Infiniti Mall in Lokhandwala, I look towards the Landmark bookshop. There are at least five men standing near its entrance. Who could they be? Sameer told me to meet him here. He had a reassuring, mature voice. But that's all I had to go by. There was no exchange of "What colour shirt are you wearing?" or any such information that could have helped us.

There's a young-looking man in a red tee and black denims standing near the aluminium-panelled column, looking out into the atrium. A middle-aged man with a long-sleeved shirt and high-waisted trousers, briefcase in hand, grinds his teeth in annoyance at something, and taps his feet restlessly. A balding middle-aged man leaning against a column near the escalator, book in hand, grey tee, blue jeans, has arms and a chest that look like they have been in the gym for quite a while.

A stylish looking middle-aged impresario with a well-cut white shirt and tapering black corduroy pants, black satchel, lounges against another column and looks around. I dial Sameer, just to see if any of these men picks up their phone.

The strong-armed man near the escalator takes out his cellphone. He's looking at me now. His eyes widen. "Hi, are you Sameer?" I ask. "Yes. I was just reading in Landmark. I always come here before going home to Virar. Did you come directly from the office?"

We move to the food court after pleasantries. He isn't one of those Bollywood hotshots with awe-inspiring schedules. Nor does he have an inflated sense of self, so common among his peers. He's earnest and straightforward about his craft.

"I'm an assistant director at Astavinayak Cine Production House here in Lokhandwala. For the big movies I tie up with the bigger houses, because that's where the money is. I help with logistics, set management, script, dialogues, location scouting and creative design. I do everything that the director can't handle. I prompt most of the actors when they forget lines during scenes. But most of the actor-interaction is done by the director. Like the character switches, etc.," he says. "I was once yelled at by an irate Gulshan Grover, who was so frustrated at getting his lines wrong that he tried to kill the messenger."

He doesn't seem to mind that the industry is still as nepotistic as it has been for decades, with an almost mafia-like hierarchy and its family-dominated monopolies. For him, working there has been a dream come true. But there are also a few traps that he hadn't expected. "For me the worst part was having people not understand my thoughts and ideas. My presentation, my…how do you say it?… diction is not up to the mark. It's a work in progress. Most directors don't give me time to discuss my ideas. I know my way around the premier production houses, but I do eventually want to make my own films," he says, good-naturedly.

"While I was in college I wanted to get into television and movies. Soon after I completed my BCom, I joined ETV in Ahmedabad a Gujarati channel with talk shows and reality shows—mostly interview-based—as an in-house director. For four years I learned all the tricks of the trade: working the cameras, editing videos, channelling the actors. I learned how to have a big say in the matter. It was a brilliant stepping stone in my career," he says. Talking about how he decided to move to Mumbai, he says, "To pursue such a career, I wanted to go to the big cities, where all the best business is. I left for Hyderabad in 2001, and worked in Film City there. It's a 30,000-acre piece of land that is used for the sole purpose of shooting. There is a mountain range inside it, and it's basically a self-sufficient world with hotels, gigantic foreign-town sets, tour buses, and the whole gig. The blessing was that I got into the position of assistant director directly, without really going through the initiation rites of being a cameraman or handyman. I learned more things, in my three years there. Hyderabad is the second largest city in India with a film industry. Then I was ready for Mumbai."

In 2004 Sameer came to Mumbai, where he was hired under a smaller director with a well-defined body of work. He learned the finer arts of film direction—the short film formats, the video-editing techniques that lent an elegant edge to the product. He also dabbled in talk shows under the Sony banner and became chief assistant director, his staple role. Meanwhile, under the guidance of his boss, he helped in the making of a bigger films called *Zindaggi Rocks*. It was his first blockbuster film. Two years later, under the roof of another production house, he helped in another film called *Luck*, and even got a cameo role in it.

It was in this production house that he found inspiration in a colleague, another associate director. Ideas that had not been entertained before went back and forth between them, a productive partnership grew, which really helped his growth as a film director.

Living as an associate director in different cities can involve mind-numbing drudgery. There is an unavoidable fatigue in trying to solve the cumbersome problems of relocation. And the work is very menial at times. But Sameer, upbringing has helped.

"My father was a bridge engineer for the western railways in India. My original hometown was Gwalior. But I only lived there for my first six years, from 1977 to 1983. Then he was transferred to Ahmedabad. That is where I lived till the end of my college life. Gwalior it being a bigger city, I made a lot of like-minded friends who had wanted to work in television and movies. About five years ago I decided to put an end to the family's nomadic lifestyle and brought them all to Mumbai: my father, mother and younger brother. We all live in a flat in Virar. I always wanted this." He smiles.

"My parents never had any issues with me choosing this as a career. My father just said, 'Make good films, make them like they do in Hollywood'," says Sameer. His father loved watching English films. "That was rare, because none of his friends watched them and he had never been in a film literate circle." Perhaps his love for cinema comes from his father.

"It was at the MAMI film festival in 2007 that I was exposed to such avant-garde cinema that it opened up my mind. I discovered directors like Polanski, Azgar Farhadi, Kurosawa, and Ang Lee. The meaning of a film changed completely for me. I realised there was so much more to it than these formula-based, hero-driven films that are raging through Bollywood. See, over the years I've noticed how actors have become kings of the movie industry here. They have a big say in how the movie will go, rather than the director. The director used to be king 20 years ago. But now it's the top 15 actors or so. The movies are built around them. And there are only a few houses that have access to them. So it's a monopoly that is discouraging for small houses like us," Sameer elaborates. "But there's also the younger generation that is realising that big-grossing films are not the only thing there should be—the IMDb generation. So we've had beautiful anomalies like *The Lunchbox* and *Ship of Theseus*, which are exactly what the industry should turn to."

So does Sameer want to break the monotony of genre in the Bollywood film industry? "Yes, I always try out these new things. I tried my hand at a short film. I watch a lot of foreign films and try to incorporate elements from them. Well, I haven't managed to succeed yet, but I'm knocking persistently on the door," he smiles. "Which is why I've been consuming a lot of knowledge of late. I've been downloading torrents of the latest foreign films. I've been reading a lot here in Landmark. I come here almost every other day to boost my zeitgeist. There is a new movement on the rise, and I want to get in on it. There are so many books that reinforce ideas I have in mind."

The last few years have seen a spurt in the number of foreign movie watchers, especially with the growth of Torrent sites that enable free and easy downloading. The piracy laws have not been tightened and there has been a lucky rampage through much of foreign indie cinema and music that have never been released in India because of tight censorship laws.

"There has been so much internal struggles, but I have come to realise that is actually a symptom of slow improvement. In the end I'm still living my dream and I haven't settled down. And that's all I need to keep myself on my toes."

Dalalstreet.com

"We always try to use natural material and ethnic textiles. The genesis and inspiration were my *dadi's* collection of gorgeous cotton saris which she brought from her tiny ancestral home when she moved to the city," says Sneha, a new age fashion entrepreneur. "We have never been to our native town in central Maharashtra, and we have no knowledge of our ancestry except these bits of cloth. Yet the threadbare material inevitably tells us the story of our generations." This connection continues to nurture as an enterprise that creatively produces contemporary designs using traditional fabric.

Mumbai has always been a city of young entrepreneurs. Dreamers have set their roots here and businesses have prospered. Sneha and Sai Nikam, sisters from Goregaon, are in the throes of setting up a brand through their online portal, "Something like Summer". And Indian textiles are used to craft these creations.

"Online portals are a better medium to set up a brand; it saves us the crazy navigation through Mumbai's realty jungle. You do have to pay for setting up the website, but in the larger scheme of things, you save a lot of money," says Sai Nikam, the younger sister who will look after management, setting of prices and handling accounts, while the elder sister, Sneha produces the designs.

It was after Sneha's brief work experience at Nor Black nor White, a tiny studio set up by a group of independent fashion entrepreneurs, that she got the idea of setting up her own business. "There I experienced a laidback work atmosphere and simultaneously a greater output, mostly because the firm worked on collaboration among friends, and thus we were far more relaxed when we bounced about ideas. I had worked at a boutique earlier, but I resented the authority and stringent work hours that came as a package with the job it offered," says Sneha, speaking for the growing number of youngsters who are stifled by the rigors of a nine-to-five job and yearn for creative freedom.

"The idea came through when we recognised how responsive Mumbai is to the idea of independent businesses. We ourselves got inspired after attending the numerous textile expos and art exhibitions happening in the city. We would love to cut up our mother's saris and incorporate them into our dresses, but she is incredibly possessive about her heirlooms," they laugh. Their home doubles up as a studio, a space littered with scraps of fabric that will later be put together into dresses and flowing tops made from ethnic materials.

The conversation takes place amidst a photo-shoot that the sisters are conducting for their website. The models showcasing their creations are friends who offered to parade the clothes for free, while being photographed by Ketan, another friend, an IT professional turned photographer. There is almost no capital that goes into the entire enterprise, and half of the budget goes into sourcing fabrics and other materials. A good part of their funds goes into travelling, as they try to imbibe the cultural aspects of the various cities in India in their designs.

Mumbai, as once was eloquently put by the author of *Tactical City*, Rupali Gupte, is Tenali Raman's city. The witty court poet of the Vijaynagara empire often used his ingenuity and adaptability to get out of tricky situations. Here, the sisters wiggle their way out of getting a professional studio to conduct their photo-shoots, by making their models pose simply on the streets near their house. A construction site becomes the perfect backdrop to set off the blue of their dresses, while a steel *patra* becomes a reflector compensating for the inadequate light. Their aim is to make fashion affordable to a wider audience.

Sai previously worked with an NGO in Dharavi to teach art and give an impetus to the artistic prowess of the children residing there. "I have actually completed my BSc with Statistics, simply because I liked the subject. Thereafter I dabbled with whatever interested me. I feel that Mumbai lets you take some time to find your way. There is no rush to take up a money making job and get into a status upholding marriage," says Sai. Working with the NGO opened her eyes to the small businesses set up in Dharavi. Some NGOs have a number of ethnic weavers who also reside in the area, specialising in Indian textiles. The sisters maintain their relationships with these organisations by sourcing fabric from them.

So far word of mouth from satisfied customers has been their best publicity. "We set up a page on Facebook, but our orders are mostly from our friends who contact their friends, who tell them about our enterprise. We even get our friends to model for us. The web is a tangled mess of upcoming brands and shocking deals, not that different from the selling scene in reality. Surviving in this business would also require ingenuity and grit, irrespective of the medium we choose," says Sneha.

Sneha and Sai represent a new trend, where commerce has shifted online. Gone are the days when you needed a physical space to sell your wares, as the virtual world is taking over the city's *dalal* streets. The luxury of managing a business from home with the comfortable click of a mouse and reduced economics, acts as a catalyst in the steady rise of online businesses. The web has become the perfect portal to shout out your interests to the world; in turn, it will embrace you with equal enthusiasm.

This is the trend in commerce, revolutionising buying and selling. Nowadays, every aspect of our daily lives, from apparel to groceries, furniture, kitchen appliances and home wares to entertainment, news, education, real estate, banking and finance, stocks and more, has successfully moved from the real space to find a bustling business street at a dot com.

Making a difference

An individual's career is, to a great extent, dependent on the person's education. Undoubtedly, education is socially and personally an indispensable part of human life. "Education helps people earn recognition and respect in society," says Kavita Rege, Principal of Saathe College for the past 12 years. She puts a lot of emphasis on education, one of the key factors that attract the city's brightest students to the excellent academic atmosphere provided by Dr Rege and her staff.

Dr Rege has had a brilliant academic career—she has a BSc and MSc from the University of Nagpur and got her PhD from the University of Mumbai. Her high intellect has been a key factor in making her what she is today. At the age of 56 she has over 30 years of teaching experience at undergraduate and postgraduate levels. "She is a very influential personality who is always there for her students," says a former student of the college.

Success didn't come easy; Dr Rege has worked hard and proved her worth. She recalls her modest upbringing in Nagpur, Maharashtra. "My parents very supportive throughout my academic career. My father was a government servant and my mother was a teacher in Nagpur," she says. Her father's demise in 1977 didn't deter her and she went on to finish her degree in MSc (Chemistry) in 1978 and earned fourth rank in the university. She was awarded a scholarship at IIT Manipur for research in Analytical Chemistry. "A scholarship of Rs 400, even at that time, wasn't enough to meet my expenses, so I decided to leave the course halfway after completing almost six months," she says.

Her career began as a Research Scientist with Alchemic Research Centre, a part of British multinational Imperial Chemical Industries. "I worked there for two years, but I was determined to finish my PhD as soon as possible," she says. Dr Rege also has valuable work experience with the Hindustan Lever Research Centre.

Accustomed to life in the slow-paced and peaceful town of Nagpur, she wanted to settle down there. But, as destiny would have it, she met her life partner, Shirish Rege, and after getting married in December 1981, they settled down in Mumbai. "It was a love-arranged marriage and surprisingly, even being from different communities, our families had no hesitation," she smiles.

One would expect a person of her stature and level of achievement—one wall of her office is adorned with the many trophies the college has won over the years—to be intimidating. But Dr Rege is a softspoken person, smiling, humble and delightful.

Having finished her MSc when she was 20, she proudly states, "I celebrated my 21st birthday in my office in Imperial Chemical Industries; I was the youngest employee there!" She went on to pursue her PhD from Mumbai University after her son and daughter were born.

Education is a big responsibility for every nation and the education of women is a must, because the empowerment and knowledge of one woman can cause a revolution in her family and society. Dr Rege is a fine example of this. She has been able to make a difference to society with her hard work and intelligence. But becoming a teacher was never on her list. It so happened that after the Reges started planning their family, she decided to work near home. Hence, she decided to apply to Saathe College for a teaching post. Now, 30 years down the line, Dr Rege is Principal.

She has always taken a keen interest in all aspects of student life at her college. "There is a strong emphasis on the overall development of a student's personality. Over the years, Saathe College has managed to produce toppers in various departments. A large number of our junior college students, especially in the humanities and commerce streams, continue their education in our degree college. Most importantly, we take care of our students and hope to inculcate in them a strong sense of values," she says.

"Initially I had stage fright; I had no experience talking to a large audience, but over the years I have overcome that." In 2009, the chief minister, in appreciation of the work being carried out by the college under the leadership of Dr Rege, awarded it Rs 50 lakhs from his fund. "Another highlight has been the 'Bharat Jodo' cycle rally from Mumbai to Jammu, organised by the college in 2009 to express solidarity with the victims of the terrorist attack on Mumbai in 2008. I am so proud of all my students who were part of that event," she says, beaming.

Besides her job as Principal, she and her husband are actively involved in the Rotary Club community service projects. Rotaract conducts many programmes and activities with a charitable purpose.

101

The Reges play a crucial part in these. Her children too have been members of the Youth Exchange Officers of the Rotary District 3014. Dr Rege has also been counsellor to a number of foreign students on the IYE exchange scheme.

An encounter with Kavita Rege makes you realise that education helps you understand yourself better and helps you realise your potential and qualities as a human being.

Fishy business

Khar Danda is a small fishing village within a relatively urbanised pocket of the city. It is modern in several ways, but when compared to its neighbours—the tall buildings of Bandra—Khar Danda looks relatively under developed. The village has a perpetual faint smell of fish lingering in the air. It isn't rare to see cats lurking and crows hovering near the entrance of the village, which has a large, airy fish market. The streets are uncomfortably dense, much like the space crunch in the city as a whole. General stores are set back and hawkers with their baskets and carts encroach upon a large part of the street. Since there is no demarcated space for a vegetable market, vendors take their business to the already packed streets. People throng the area in the evening to buy groceries, making driving through the village difficult and noisy. In the midst of this chaos, a number of small, primarily fish-related businesses thrive.

At a short distance from the crowded village, the landscape begins to change, giving way to open spaces, with poles for drying fish and shacks with small yards. In one of these yards, Aziz *bhai* watches as two men fill baskets with dry fish waste. "No, I don't sell fish," he says.

"I buy the dry fish waste from these fishermen. They sort it and pack it for me."

The yard is covered with piles of dry fish, indistinguishable from the waste when seen from afar. That's where the sorters come in. Two women gingerly sort the dry fish into three piles: one for prawns, one for edible fish and a third for inedible fish and other waste. The fishermen hire them for the job. A man supervises the work; it is his fish being sorted and sold. Fishing is his family business. Also in the yard is a large strainer with fish stuck to it. It looks like a sieve used at construction sites.

"I pay Rs 290 per basket for this. What's waste to them is very valuable to me. I run a manure business and use this fish waste to make manure. We then sell it to bigger companies like Godrej and Wipro, who add chemicals to it and sell it commercially. I run this business with my brother, Anif," Aziz says. The business is particularly interesting because what we think is useless waste can actually spawn or sustain a business. A fish passes through the hands of several people before it reaches the plate. This forms a huge network that deals with fishing related activities: fishermen, wholesalers, retailers, sorters, etc. This branches off into smaller businesses that meet other businesses of the city at their nodes. Aziz *bhai's* business is one such link in the network, dealing with the drying, sorting and selling of fish. The structure of this network is interesting because everyone benefits from it.

Apart from his manure business, Aziz *bhai* also owns a poultry farm. His father came from Saurashtra, Gujarat, and started the business after he quit his job. Aziz *bhai* and Anif have been running both the businesses. A resident of Versova, Aziz *bhai* works from Madh Island and travels to Khar Danda to buy fish waste from the fishermen who sell their fish to retailers, who in turn sell it in a fish market, or go from door to door, selling it at higher prices.

What is fascinating about this is how the fishermen intelligently profit by selling both fish and the waste that comes from it, and how a single industry can cause people of seemingly unrelated business backgrounds and from different parts of the city to cross paths.

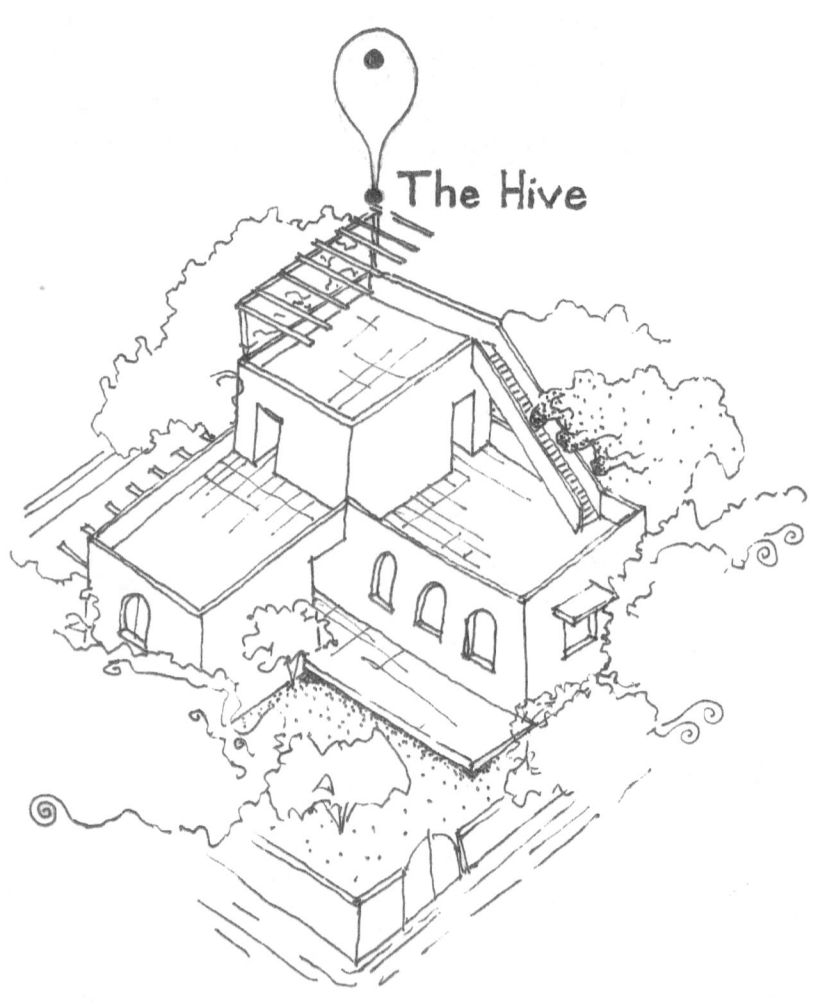

The Hive

The Hive

Mumbai's prosperity and employment generating potential attracts migrants from across the country. Once a textile manufacturing hub, the city's socio-economic structure has witnessed a sea change due to a paradigm shift in business activities dominated by entrepreneurial spirit. These days, a new business owner in the country is less driven by profit and economics and more by passion. Thus, the nature of business is changing, as is its structural organisation. The emergence of technology like smartphones, high speed Internet connections, etc., has changed the concept of formal office spaces, freelancers, startups and small businesses now enjoy the freedom to work from anywhere. This answers questions about the rise in numbers of collaborative work spaces in the city that not only provide the tools needed to work, but also create networking opportunities that ultimately lead to growth. One such trending spot is 'The Hive'.

In a narrow lane in Chuim Village, Bandra, opposite the tiny Ahmed Bakery sits Huma Mansion, an old Portuguese bungalow echoing tales of foreign influence in the city. This rundown structure was transformed into a cool multidisciplinary space called The Hive, leased and run by Cultural Shoq in late 2013. Strolling through the back lanes here, one cannot help but notice how the bold graffiti on the compound wall announces a different world that is inside. The back gate opens into a semi-open area with lots of plants and a few tables and chairs; it looks like a café. There is a girl sitting there, busy working on her laptop. When asked about the person in charge, she points towards a door and says, "Sudeip is in there." The door opens into a room that seems soundproof, with its acoustically treated walls. A man who seems to be in his early 30s, dressed casually in a T-shirt and pants, greets the visitors with a warm smile. "Welcome to The Hive," says Sudeip Nair, the founder, with a firm handshake.

Sudeip started working on The Hive in 2009, and moved to the present location in late 2013'. Before setting up Hive, Sudeip had co-founded The Bombay Elektrik Project, famed for organising music events, poetry slams and film screenings.

"All of this began with the thought of setting up a platform for upcoming artistes," says Sudeip. A Malayalee, he was born and brought up in Bangalore. Later, a new job opportunity took his father, who worked in advertising, to Mumbai, and the family moved there in 1997. "We stayed in Four Bungalows, Andheri West, initially. Even though I've lived in other metros like Bangalore and Hyderabad, shifting to Mumbai gave me a major cultural shock. Until I came here, I never really understood what people meant when they called it 'the city that never sleeps'. It was fascinating to see a city brimming with so much energy!"

He explains, "Over the years, an interesting thing that I've noticed about Mumbai is that it has an equal ratio of people doing nine-to-five jobs and entrepreneurs. Be it in any field, the city is home to all kinds of entrepreneurs, from the small *chaiwalla* and vegetable vendors on the streets to the big and established businessmen." Sudeip, who is from an arts background and a graduate in hotel management from IHM, Aurangabad, decided to set up Bombay Elektrik Project to try his luck in the city. It was around this time that Sudeip noticed the lack of venues supporting experimental art. "The Hive" was launched as an integrated urban centre for art and technology.

"It provides one of the best support structures for the creative community. A space that combines four different activities: work, entertainment, education and food," Sudeip says proudly.

Hive has different sections to support these functions. "The Xircus", is a 50-seater soundproof room for the performing arts. Nearby is "The Workshop", with mirrored walls, designed for workshops on dance, acting, etc. The last of the dedicated areas on the ground level is "The Hungry Traveller", an organic café. With wooden tables, folding wrought-iron chairs and tables, the canteen is open for chefs to experiment with new recipes and get an immediate response. "The Collab", a collaborative space for science lovers, with specially designed tables, is split in two levels and can be rented out as per requirements. The Hive also has two open terraces that can be leased out for open-air performances. With walls adorned with murals and paintings by local artists, the space is truly a hive of cultural and artistic bees.

"The Hive has been shaped purely by the way Mumbai works. The new entrepreneurs in the city demanded a space to develop their ideas and, unlike many other collaborative work spaces in the city, we just tried to make them comfortable," Sudeip says. This explains why The Hive is pet friendly—it's probably the only office that welcomes non-human babies.

This is one among the many collaborative working spaces in the city that aid the young, vibrant population keen to work differently. The present generation demands flexible spaces that provide them with various options—hubs to enjoy the perks of an office, minus the boss!

Through the prayer flags

"When I lived in Calcutta, often when I walked down the street, a rowdy bunch of children would sneak up to me, shout 'Chini Chong' and run away. It is the same for all of us, with Mongoloid features, wherever we go in India," says Mr Wangchuk, who runs Sernyaa, the only Tibetan restaurant in Mumbai. He also goes by the name of Uncle Sylvester, as he is tired of people mispronouncing his name. He shares the plight of numerous Indians who leave behind the pristine mountains in the north-eastern states to reside in the plains.

"You get used to it; there is nothing that you can do. Reconciling is the only thing that we can do. We cannot run behind those kids all day." He serves up what he calls his truly authentic *jasha momos*. Sernyaa, which is Tibetan for goldfish, is a small hole-in-the-wall eatery in the predominantly Muslim area of Oshiwara. Mr Wangchuk sits on a the bench outside his tiny restaurant with its predominantly red interiors. Red is the colour of preservation and life force in Tibetan Buddhism. "My forefather came from Tibet long before the invasion. We lived in Sikkim and I consider myself

111

Sikkimese. I am an Indian, and I will assert this over and over again. Around 1980 I started living in China Pada in Calcutta." China Pada literally means "Chinese colony", which is offensive because the residents there are mostly Tibetans or northeast Indians, and have almost nothing in common with the Chinese.

"I completed my degree from IHM Kolkata and worked at Taj Bengal for some time, after which I was transferred to Taj Mumbai. It was there that I worked with Sanjeev Kapoor, but later branched out to set up Sernyaa, as I wanted to get Tibetan food to people who had never experienced it," says Mr Wangchuk, as he asks us to taste his spicy Tibetan seaweed creation. "All these dishes are my grandmother's creations. She left me a bible of sorts of authentic Tibetan recipes that I simply follow." His love for food is evident as he regales us with the recipe for the perfect chilli chicken, and the different varieties of soy.

He talks about the difficulties of serving an ethnic cuisine in a city that knows nothing about it. "We have had to add Chinese recipes to the menu because our customers are usually perplexed when faced with a strongly Tibetan menu. Also, Buddhism doesn't allow the serving of fish, but we serve it to provide options to people who may not understand our religious leanings. Mumbai is a gourmet lover's city, but so much of the food scene is still left unexplored." A framed portrait of the Dalai Lama hangs on the wall, even though Mr Wangchuk follows the Karma Kagyu sect of Buddhism. There are also a number of knick-knacks from Tibet, like a golden dangling chandelier of fish, an auspicious Buddhist symbol which completes the Tibetan vibe.

"There are very few Tibetans living in Mumbai and we meet only during Losar (New Year)." He dreams of opening a Tibetan style pub in the near future. "It will have peaceful music, a place where families can come and dine. And the alcohol served will be Chang, Ara and other north-eastern specialties." He says this with infectious optimism.

It is truly a constructed reality, when an exiled community attempts to build a home away from home with elements from their past intermarrying with local realities and modern amenities. Maybe the sound of dungchens will echo through the air, with snow-capped peaks in the background and maroon robed monks dotting the hillside. Perhaps the music will be pre-recorded, and the mountains just in posters on the wall, but close your eyes and maybe you will be transported to Mr Wangchuk's Shangri-la. And then his dream will have become reality.

Circulating happiness

The walls of the shop are completely hidden by books stacked from floor to ceiling—magazines, comics and bestsellers at the front, children's books further inside, classics, romance novels, thrillers, self-help and just about every type of book imaginable. A narrow passage loops around the long shop, with a bookshelf with more books running along the middle. The waft of old books often entices the passing book lover into the store. NA Merchant sits at his counter at the front, looking out at the busy street leading to the busy Sitladevi temple junction in Mahim. He has one eye on his small CCTV screen, monitoring all the activity behind the many stacks. The shelves behind him are filled with hundreds of DVDs, just below a sign that reads 'No Credit—Fixed Rate'.

With television and the Internet for competition, people find it hard in today's fast paced life to find time to relax with a good book. The Victoria Music House and Circulating Library is one of the few of its kind left in the city; happily, the number of its patrons has slowly been increasing over the years. Its location next to a bus-stop on busy Lady Jamshedji Road between Victoria

Church and the Sitladevi temple, ensures that many people walk past it regularly.

With a monthly membership fee of Rs 250, it is a good deal for avid readers and film buffs living in the area. While the book rental business has been on a rise over the years, movie DVD lending is far more lucrative for Merchant, accounting for 75 percent of his business. The DVDs occupy just a fraction of the space in the library; books fill up the rest. "This is the main reason many other circulating libraries of old times have turned into purely movie rental businesses," explains Merchant. "Everyone is aware of how valuable a small space in Mumbai is."

Merchant's father, AJ Merchant was a soap dealer and owned a large shop next to the Sitladevi temple. Seeing his two sons' growing fascination with comic books, he decided to try selling those as well. He set up a comic book stand and found that they sold very quickly. By 1950, AJ Merchant had phased out soap, and begun a small-scale comic book store and book rental service.

His sons expanded the rental business over time and set up a circulating library. They divided the space into two parts—one half was rented to a laundry and dry cleaning service for extra income, and the other half became a library. Today, NA Merchant is "semi-retired" and spends some afternoons at the library when his son, who is otherwise in charge, is away. The library itself has been divided into three, one part each for Merchant's brother and his two sons.

From his seat behind the counter, Merchant watches the traffic and people passing by. "Bombay is growing so quickly," he says. "I remember when there were only a few cars on the street and most people would walk or take a bus. Now everyone wants to ride in

115

their own car. People are getting used to a faster life; you can watch a film in two hours, or you can take ten days to read the same story in a book."

He smiles, "Today youngsters are also more 'free'. They are not tied back as we were years ago. Even books are changing with the times—to put it bluntly, books are more 'sexy' now; no one is shocked by them, like before. Those taboo days are over and people are openly enjoying reading them!"

Merchant's childhood fascination with comics has not faded. Now a passionate old comic-book collector, he has over 5,000 at home, apart from collections of newer prints in the library. An ardent DC and Marvel comics fan, he does not care much for Indian publications, and stocks only a few. He also enjoys the pop culture Archie comics, which he relates to the liberated youth of Mumbai today.

As a purist, Merchant loathes the newer styles of comic-book art. "They are so messy," he says, opening a Flash Gordon comic from a pile nearby. "It's hard to find Flash in these confusing drawings." Pointing to another comic in the pile, he says, "*Arre baap re*, look, they have made Batman look so ugly! *Shee shee...*"

Merchant wants to share his collection with other enthusiasts, but the books are too rare and too valuable to keep at the shop. He says, "All the good old-time comics have been bought by collectors, who keep them safe where no one else can see them." Merchant hopes to soon start an old comic-book collectors, club and organise meetings at the Victoria Library. He will then be able to share his all-time favourite superhero, Captain Marvel with a younger, deprived generation. "*Captain Marvel* was published only from 1940 to 1952," he explains. "DC Comics claimed that the character was a copy of its main superhero, Superman. They won their case against Marvel and sadly, the production of the comic was discontinued. It was a very good comic."

Another of his most prized comic books is *The Death of Superman*. "The story is so touching; it brings tears to my eyes even when I read it now." He is jolted out of his fantasy world by a customer, a man looking to rent a couple of Bollywood movie DVDs. Before Merchant has finished picking them off the shelf, another customer enters and asks for a self-help book. Merchant calls out to his assistants. The evening gets busier and Merchant, drawn away from his comic books, concentrates instead on making entries he makes in his small exercise book, tallying deposit amounts and late-returned fees.

Dream.Believe.Achieve

In the myriad bylanes of Bhuleshwar he stands out in his spotless white *kurta* amidst the colourful beads in his shop. Ravindra Kisanlal Gandhi, 72, is a successful businessman, a wholesale seller of beads and small artefacts. He owns two shops, a few godowns and a couple of properties in the crowded lanes of the precinct. Most people know this area for the famous Zaveri Bazaar, Crawford Market and Chor Bazaar.

Ravindra belongs to a small town in Gujarat called Unjhathat, famous for its cumin seeds and psyllium (or isabgol) market. Although today he has made a fortune for himself and his family, his journey as a trader hasn't been easy.

"I lost my mother at the age of two and was sent to live with my maternal uncle for a while," explains Ravindra. During his stay in Visnagar in Mehsana district of Gujarat, he learned that his father had remarried. "When I went back to live with my father, my life wasn't the same. My stepmother really ill-treated me. When I was 13, I had a fight with my father and that was the last straw. I left him and my stepmother and decided to go my own way," Ravindra says.

It was an incredibly risky decision to take at that age, but he does not regret it one bit. "Nor do I hold anything against my father. All the risks I've taken in my life so far have been because of my decision to leave home, and I am who I am today because of those risks. I'm very grateful for whatever has happened to me."

When faced with adversity, it is hard to dream big. After leaving his father's house, Ravindra moved in with an uncle who stayed in Mumbai's CP Tank area. Along with cooking and other household chores, he worked as a helper in his uncle's shop. "I was like a servant there, but I am thankful to him for allowing me to stay in his house," he recalls.

After gathering some money, Ravindra set up his own stall outside a shop, selling beads, *rakhis* and pearls. Even though fear and anxiety gripped him, he knew he had to begin somewhere, no matter how small. His passion for a better livelihood gave him clarity of thought and lifted his spirits. It also helped him create a vision for a better future. It was his commitment and relentless hard work that got him all the success he's earned today.

Over the years he earned enough money to buy a shop of his own and continue his business on a larger scale. At the age of 28, Ravindra found a life partner in his best friend, Rekha. She was his lucky charm, not just in his personal life, but also in his professional life. His business grew tremendously after their marriage and in 1968 he established the RT Company at Bhuleshwar. Their initial business plan was to sell *rakhis* in bulk. He would get all the raw material from Kolkata and they would stay awake for several nights to make the rakhis, even pulling in their children, Sandeep and Deepali.

"It was getting exhausting month after month, but I never lost hope," Ravindra says with a smile. Most people who come to

Mumbai have big dreams, but face bigger obstacles. Many of those dreams don't survive the cruelty of the city, but backed with sincere passion and undying hope, dreams like Ravindra's can be realised.

The markets of Bhuleshwar evolved with time and as competition increased, Ravindra decided to shift his focus from *rakhis* to beads, pearls, decorative items, fancy candles and the like. "Today, I have over 10,000 different products to sell," he boasts, displaying his colourful range of plastic beads.

His son, Sandeep, joined the business and expanded it. For the past couple of years, he has been travelling to China to buy beads and sell them in bulk in the Indian market. "He is very smart and has good business sense," Ravindra says with pride in his voice. "He wanted to expand the business, so I gave him a part of the shop and let him do what he wanted. He needs guidance once in a while, which is when I step in. Apart from that, I do not interfere in his work and he doesn't in mine."

He says humbly, "These streets of Bhuleshwar have become my home. But I've never forgotten my roots. I have never let anything get to my head, neither the poverty that engulfed me earlier in my life, nor the wealth I have now."

A responsible and gracious man, Ravindra gives back to society in his own way. Along with money, he donates stationery, books and a lot of his time to needy children, hoping to provide a better life for them.

He knows he has a lot of people to thank and he is especially grateful for the reliable and loyal workers who have become a part of his business over the past 40 years. "Trust is the key to any business and my motto in life has and always will be: Dream, believe, achieve!"

The invisible visible

Nestled between the high rises of Nariman Point in our "gen-next" city, it is a rare to sight a *mela*. In the midst of laughter and the playful squeals of children at the Chacha Nehru Baal Mela resides a unique family that runs the fair. Heading them is a woman whom everyone seems to know—vendors, children and parents alike—giving her the aura of power and influence. This is Indu Palani, a social worker of an unusual sort.

Dressed in a simple yet elegant sari, her hair neatly tied in a bun and her delicate ears trying to bear the weight of her heavy earrings, Indu is a sight to behold. "In the early 1970s, I came with my parents from Solapur to Mumbai, then called Bombay, after three consecutive years of a devastating drought in Maharashtra," she says. She was just a child then and has come a long way since. Today she holds the post of secretary at the *mela*.

"My parents were caretakers, responsible for storing grains in our village," Indu reminisces as she watches the kids play. "We would get a year's supply of grains in return for keeping them safely. Then the droughts hit, at the same time as the Indo-Pak War of 1971. Lack of sufficient rainfall in Solapur resulted in my parents losing their jobs. When they heard about Mumbai being the land of opportunity, a city where no poor person goes to bed hungry, they decided to get all of us here."

Indu explains, "Clueless but full of hope, my parents and eight of us kids travelled by train to Mumbai. We got off at Kalyan station, as we didn't have the tickets for the journey ahead. My father convinced my mother to walk the rest of the journey out of fear of being pulled up by a ticket collector. The walk was so long and our resources so limited that my father eventually resorted to begging so he could get us food and water. I remember walking, holding my siblings' hands, taking every painful step ahead; we were completely exhausted, physically and financially. That was our journey to Mumbai!"

On the way, one of Indu's sisters was injured by stray nails on the railway tracks. Laid low by exhaustion and lack of medical care, she passed away. Her death added to the miserable plight of the homeless family, already intimidated by the city. However, taking one step at a time, her parents set out looking for employment.

"My parents happened to meet a *thekedaar* called Razak*bhai* who operated near Marine Lines in those days. They got work as labourers at a construction site and we all moved into a shack on the site, which became our home," says Indu. After each project was completed they had to relocate to another site.

Indu recalls what her father often told her. "The *thekedaars* paid the workers for six days of work out of seven, to ensure they didn't run away once the week was over." Just as today there are certain pick-up points in the city where workers go in search of daily wages, workers in her parents' time would gather near Oval Maidan and wait for a *thekedaar* to give them work."

This stability was only temporary. Being exposed to hazardous living and working conditions, Indu's parents soon started falling ill. Like many poor and ignorant migrants in the city, they could not afford medical treatment. "When I was 15, my mother died from tuberculosis. For my dad, who was already physically weak, the news of my mother's death was a huge shock. He left us and never returned."

As the eldest of the siblings, the task of taking care of her six brothers fell on Indu's shoulders. Since they could not live at the construction site anymore, this clueless bunch of children often slept on the platforms at Churchgate station. "I have spent sleepless nights guarding my brothers and myself from all sorts of people," Indu says as she recounts the horrors of being homeless. "Some would be drunk, some were eve teasers, some harassed us and hit us."

It was hard. "Initially, I begged at traffic signals to feed my siblings. Soon my brothers also joined me," says Indu. The desire to earn a living beyond just making ends meet inspired Indu to search for options. She began selling toys and making *gajras*. "I would wake up at 4 am and stand at Lion Gate (an entry to Mumbai docks) for hours to get work. If I didn't get any work there, I would continue making *gajras* and selling them all day. At times, I would even work as a maid in people's homes. As all of us siblings grew older, we started taking up work at construction sites at Matunga, Panvel, Dadar and Elphinstone, among others."

With perseverance, things started to look better. "My brothers became strong enough to handle things on their own. Now some of them sell coconut water, while others work at construction sites, and my youngest brother is still living with me," says Indu.

At 17, Indu married a construction worker, continuing to live at various construction sites. She gave birth to two girls, and not wanting them to suffer the same ordeals, she wanted to educate them. Let alone support her, her husband turned to alcohol and drugs. Things got so bad that Indu had to take the difficult decision of leaving him, and took her daughters along.

Continuing as a daily wager, she once again tried to stabilise her life. This is when she met her second husband. He worked at the *mela*, and introduced Indu to the colourful and lively life of the fair. Initially she was merely a vendor selling toys and other knick-knacks. But slowly the *mela* became a huge part of her life. Given the hardships she faced, Indu decided to help other unemployed people by providing them with various odd jobs at the *mela* like selling balloons, bubbles and toys, feeding and cleaning the horses, riding the chariots, etc. It's been seven years at the *mela*, and Indu has diligently and painstakingly built a new family of opportunities.

There are around 130 families who are dependent on the *mela* and the people who visit are really supportive. Indu recalls, "Once a case was filed against us claiming cruelty against animals, specifically for the removal of the horses that pulled the chariots. At that hour of need, the patrons stood by us. We have always treated our horses like our children. We even have a vet appointed to take care of them and give them tetanus injections twice a year. Didn't people realise there were so many families who were attached to and dependent on those horses? Taking away the chariots might force many to resort to illegal ways of money making—something that we at the *mela* have always fought against." Indu believes that opportunities like these can give the poor a chance to a better life.

The *mela* is also facing pressures of redevelopment. "On one side are the upper-class people who keep filing court cases about animal rights, noise regulations, etc., and on the other, the builders who want to redevelop our slums and try to force us to vacate our homes in exchange for money or by providing us with flats of lesser area than promised," says Indu, agitatedly.

There exist, almost invisibly in our city, many people like Indu and events like Chacha Nehru Baal Mela, thriving on relationships and opportunities within the visible fabric of Mumbai. Perhaps the potential of a butterfly effect makes them an integral part of a society, a city, a state, a country and the world!

dream
believe
achieve

Sounds of change

When I was 8, I remember stepping through a doorway into a large shop, its musty interior filled with music books in dusty plastic covers and a few pianos and other instruments covered with white sheets to keep them free of dust. The ghostly and intimidating atmosphere was broken abruptly by the sounds of a lone customer trying out a piano—a happy sound that instantly turned the space from morbid to merry.

Today, I step through the same doorway, into the Furtados piano showroom in Jer Mahal, as a doorman holds open the glass door. He takes my bag at the entrance and hands me a token. The swanky interior lined with shiny new imported Steinway pianos and buzzing with activity is quite different from my childhood memories of the same space. The one common element, however, is the well-rounded figure of Anthony Gomes, assisting his customers with the same enthusiasm and courtesy that defined him 18 years ago.

Anthony reveals that Furtados has been witnessing change—as has the entire western music industry in Mumbai—for a very long time now. Before independence, western music in India flourished under British rule. St Xavier's and several other schools and colleges had full-fledged music education departments and took great pride in their orchestra groups.

The 1950s, however, saw a complete purging of western music, with the new Indian government wanting as few reminders of the British as possible. Music education programmes were scrapped and western music in the city waned to almost nothing.

"The Furtado family, which owned two stores of musical instruments in Jer Mahal, found its profits declining and decided to sell one of its stores. 'BXFurtado', the store named after Bernard Xavier Furtado, was sold to my father John Gomes in 1953," says Anthony.

The second store, "LMFurtado", named after Louis Manoel Furtado, was auctioned by the Collector of Mumbai in 1959 when its owner, George Selwyn migrated to Canada. John Gomes bid for it and won, thus becoming the owner of both stores.

Until the 1980s the clientele at the Furtados shops was limited to musicians from communities that had been heavily influenced by the British—the Parsis and the Christians. The last 20 years, though, have seen increasingly diverse communities drawn towards western music.

"Until 1994, prior to liberalisation of the Indian economy, there was a complete embargo on imports. The instruments that Furtados sold were either second-hand or domestically produced, which could not compare to the quality standards and sound of their western counterparts," recalls Anthony.

In spite of this, Furtados was the only go-to place for musicians then. Apart from instrument sales, the company organised events and coordinated the Trinity College of London music exams for the few people in the city who studied music with private tutors.

After the economy was thrown open—starting from the late 1990s—things started changing gradually. Now with more people taking to western music once again, well-made pianos are being imported and the demand for them is increasing.

The change has been very gradual though, due to the dearth of infrastructure for western music in the city. While interest has been piqued, schools to learn music and auditoria to showcase talent are limited.

Yet, Mumbai is at the forefront of western music in India. The National Centre for Performing Arts (NCPA) is the only theatre in the country that is fully equipped for a classical western music recital.

Anthony Gomes and his three siblings are doing plenty to improve this further. Apart from widening instrument ranges, they started an annual event called "Con Brio" in 2010—a piano competition and festival to develop the art in India, with concerts, master classes, workshops and a residential piano camp. In 2011, they started the "Furtados School of Music" to make classical western music education more accessible, and in 2012 they opened the "Furtados Institute of Piano Technology", a long-term project to train piano tuners and technicians.

The Gomes family has kept the faith in the business of western music over the years, and today their efforts are paying off as profits are rising. They began expanding to other cities in 2007, with branches opening in Goa, Delhi, Bangalore, and Pondicherry. They now have 21 showrooms across the country.

Renting instruments and sound equipment is also a profitable part of their business, with more international artists visiting the city to perform every year. Furtados supports non-commercial concerts and college music events as well by sponsoring the equipment. They support the younger generation's enthusiasm in all kinds of western music, be it classical, jazz, blues or rock.

At the piano showroom, once the LMFurtado store, Anthony Gomes walks over to assist a South Indian family choosing a piano for their home. The bespectacled son, about 10 years old, plays a Schubert piece flawlessly, while his parents discuss the pianos and their cost with Anthony.

Synapses within

The city has always been divided into sectors owned by the government, individuals or some faction of society. An architect happened to mention that while mapping these various fractions, the BMC sometimes chances upon slivers of land owned by nobody. Some tiny bit is left without an owner, and they imagine that land to be a desolate barren space without a soul in sight. But in reality, these slivers are occupied and bustling with life, and are as much a part of the city as the ubiquitous landmarks of Mumbai.

One such sliver is Bhangarwada in Malad, wherein resides a strictly Tamilian population of sweepers, housemaids, drivers and the like. The roads are clogged with shanties spilling out onto them, and there is always a loudspeaker blaring remixed Tamil songs. The community has its own temple with a *gopuram*, its own wedding hall and its own share of independent businesses and tiny enterprises. The area organises its own 10-feet *Ganapatimandal* and its own processions during Onam and other religious festivals, but the entire community occupies less than a 700m long road jampacked with shanties.

One such is home to Sarasvati, who works as a housemaid at a tower nearby. She came to Mumbai in the 1990s, and it was a decision she made on her own, forcing her husband to comply. "Our small village in Tamil Nadu was in a drought-prone area. There was not even a drop of water available. I came from a family of farmers who had to watch their crops fail due to lack of irrigation. In fact, a tap was installed in our village only last year," she laments. "Here in our small shanty, even though we don't have water 24/7, we can store enough water to last us a day. We don't have to travel miles to get water, it is available in our taps."

She remembers, "I got married into a house with all the facilities except water. It was a proper brick house, unlike the temporary shelter we have here. But sometimes all these riches without the essentials are of no use." Her fingers are chafed and raw from washing dishes in four houses every day, but she maintains that it's a job of dignity. "There were no opportunities to work in my village. Here, there is a job for everyone who is willing to work. I can let go of one job and know with assurance that I can get another," she says in another ode to the City of Opportunity.

Her three daughters are currently studying in schools—the eldest is pursuing higher studies. "I started working as a maid because that was the only thing I knew. I have never let my daughters out to work and I never will. They will study and make a name for themselves, something that I could not do because I received no education."

She talks about the community life of Bhangarwada, of the festivals and the animosity lurking within. "Of course there is rivalry—we are all maids. There is constant competition about who scores the most houses to work in, and who clinches the most pay. It is the same in the rich houses I work in, except that they deal with a larger sum of money and poorer values. Even though we fight, we know that we have to stick together. We are all from the same land, have the same complexion and speak the same language. It is apparent that we have to stick together. There are a number of such communities around Mumbai, and we try to maintain relationships with them too."

Sarasvati is a self-sufficient woman who at times earns more than her husband does. Yet she prefers the squalor of Mumbai to her village. There is a satisfaction that she feels she has achieved through hard physical labour and a certain contentment that allows her to sleep comfortably under her tin roof at night.

A synapse is the slim space between two nerve endings, a seemingly empty space across which signals are transmitted. It is this void that holds the nervous system together and enables the body to function. And in this city, it is in those slivers where a population holds the city together.

The scion

"My grandfather had been a *sarpanch*, championing our village's progressive situation, getting clinics, hospitals, bus-stops and concreted-roads ready for the post-1980 spurt of technological increment," says Nilesh in slightly accented English, smartly dressed in a striped shirt and black trousers, sitting on the sofa in the lobby of Johnson & Johnson. "He was venerated for years in my village, but after he died, our social status decayed. Though the family was full of relatively well-educated ex-farmers like doctors and engineers, after him there was no one else in such a strategic position in governance."

In 1980, Nilesh was born into the wealthy Mahajan family of Jalgaon, of the clan of the old Levapatels of the Deccan, a year after his paternal grandfather died suddenly, unexpectedly. "The Mahajans' political clout further thawed under the heat of a legal enforcement that reduced their 800-acre property to 100 acres. The shell-shocked siblings had to settle for even smaller, meagre portions," explains Nilesh. "Soon we started looking towards the metropolis for new opportunities. But it was not easy for our parents' generation to migrate."

Since Nilesh's maternal grandparents stayed in the police quarters at Dadar, he visited Mumbai regularly during vacations. For the young Nilesh it was the city of dreams. "I always loved Mumbai. The locality I stayed in, my friends, everything.... For a few years I did my schooling in Mumbai, staying with my grandparents. However, when I was 10 I met with a small accident during the festivities of Holi; my grandparents freaked and sent me back to Jalgaon," remembers Nilesh. "It was a sad change. For the next decade I was schooled in the somewhat backward system where boys and girls don't sit together, (because of) inequality among classmates and all that ultra-conservative jazz."

Nilesh always wanted to get that spark back and professional education seemed to be his next chance. "It was then that I realised how financially poor we had become. When the moment came for me to choose a college on the computerised seat-allocation rounds, my high merit marks had earned me the choice of four of the best pharmacy colleges in Mumbai. When I conferred with my uncle there, he told me to choose the smallest one in Faizpur, a small town just outside Jalgaon, because my father wouldn't be able to afford the expensive Mumbai college fees." And it was in Faizpur that Nilesh finally found that elusive bonhomie he had been part of at his grandparents' home in Dadar.

"It was a group of five of us, two girls and three guys. We were all from different backgrounds; three of them came from Mumbai. I finally had a gang of friends; it blotted out all those lonely high school years and the disappointment of not getting to Mumbai. There was everything: concocting juvenile start-up companies with the guys, talking about personal ambitions and the distant future, love, friendship; I was very emotional about it."

When he finally graduated six years later in 2005, he realised that the pressures his old parents lived with had taken a toll on them. His father had even taken on previously-unheard-of alternatives like raising money by driving a rickshaw. It was a rude awakening of sorts and it led to introspection: "I wanted to do an MBA, I wanted to give the GRE, I wanted to go abroad but, as always, the money was too much. Old dreams were dying slowly. One day my old principal, anticipating all this in his head, came to my rescue. He offered to pay for my Masters in Pharmacy," remembers Nilesh of his strong ally. "It was a Rs 44,000-a-semester thing. I did not hesitate, and I wasn't ashamed. But when I called him to ask him for help regarding my sister's wedding payments—which is a tiresome communal tradition of indulgence—I felt very, very cheap indeed."

He began his affair with Mumbai in 2006, as a sales representative responsible for selling pharmaceuticals to medical practitioners in the city. He switched to the field of clinical research a year later, and got into the hallowed echelons of drug development. Simultaneously he studied for his PhD in Faizpur, financed by his principal, travelling on weekends to his hometown to work on his thesis with his guide. "Once I got my PhD, I knew I would be relatively better off than many people at getting a job within the city." Bayer, another multi-national pharmaceutical was conquered in 2009, and in 2011 Nilesh got into the implacable Johnson & Johnson. "Here I handle a national unit concerned with R&D for medical machinery. I have a huge say in the matter. It's big."

He is proud, but there are problems. "Whenever I go back to Jalgaon, once a month, it sickens me how the place has fallen apart.

Our place. The Mahajan' properties. All my relatives who have drifted apart have lost our original splendour. Heck, I guess we were all to blame. We didn't stick together. But many of them are here, stronger and better." So what does his new "hometown" Mumbai have to offer him for the future? The place he'd always dreamed of living in, surrounded by warmth and lights and cacophonous bonhomie?

"I lost a lot of freedom in the pursuit of happiness. This is all from the money I've earned in this city." He gesticulates, moving his hands to signify the bigness of the space. "I have everything that could run my family, my wife who is a former colleague, and my old parents whom I've brought to my house in Thane.... Because at the end of the day, it does make it easier: money," he grins.

"I think that I have had so many dreams stuck in the pipeline that I would like to restart some. I have a desire to explore other countries. I want to try out hobbies that were only luxuries before. Photography is one. Painting is another," says Nilesh. With new processes in education, governance and economy burgeoning, the rigidity of yesteryear India is slowly softening and high-performing individuals like him are seeking out the unorthodox. Opportunities are ubiquitous, and Nilesh is taking whatever comes his way. "This place is now a base from where I can live and plan. Plans for the future. I am always meeting new people. Finding out more about the corporate world. I want to build my resources. I think of moving abroad temporarily. Let's see. I'm now in a good position."

As he walks to the elevators that lead to his high-end office, I realise that he is no longer clutching at a straw of hope, but has reached the place of intermediate rest before he takes on the summit.

Whispers children shouldn't hear

She rubbed her puffy eyes, smudging the black kohl she had meticulously applied the previous evening before business hours started. Her eyes were swollen from lack of sleep—the previous night she had been busy satisfying the carnal needs of various men. She is Lakshmi, one of the thousands of prostitutes who live in "the tainted" lanes of Kamathipura, struggling to survive.

The soft filtered rays of the rising sun light her face as she describes her life in Kamathipura, Mumbai's oldest and largest red-light area. Kamathipura attained its name from the *kamathis* (workers) of Andhra Pradesh, who were labourers on the construction sites of the causeways that connected the former seven islands of Bombay in 1795.

In this red-light district, an estimated 100,000 brothels house sex workers, most of whom are not here voluntarily. A very high proportion of women and girls are sold or bartered into the flesh trade, often by a trusted family member or distant relative; others are, born into it. These narrow lanes running parallel to each other have an air of normalcy during the day, with people working in their shops and standing at corner *paan* shops having discussions.

"At night, these lanes turn into a place of sexual fantasies and forbidden pleasures," says Lakshmi. Evenings, prostitutes can be seen outside their brothels, compelled to wear bright red lipstick, garish makeup and tight tops with jeans or tight skirts to lure customers. On the balconies of the buildings men can be seen taking their pick and striking a deal or bargaining for prices and timings.

Surprisingly, Lakshmi is in the flesh trade voluntarily. "After my husband died in 2005, my life came crashing down. I was left clueless, with two kids to nurture," she explains, swallowing unshed tears. Originally from Kuara village in West Bengal, after the unfortunate and sudden demise of her husband, Lakshmi came to Mumbai along with her two sons. She did not have any real family in West Bengal, apart from a few unfriendly relatives. The mystical allure of Mumbai grabbed her attention and she decided to start afresh. "I didn't want my young sons to live a life of poverty. I wanted them to be educated and fulfil their aspirations," she says.

On her arrival in Mumbai, she made a few acquaintances; one of them was Rashmi, who gave her the idea of making quick money by entering the flesh trade in the red-light area of Kamathipura. It was an idea that Lakshmi easily brushed off, saying, "Have you lost your mind!" But after many failed attempts at finding a job, desperation got the better of her and she was left with no other option but to enter prostitution and earn her living.

"Life here is incredibly difficult. Poverty, drugs and alcohol addiction, gambling and violence are an everyday reality. We are frowned upon and ignored by the so-called literate part of society," Lakshmi says matter-of-factly. It is estimated that around

50 per cent of Indian sex workers are HIV-positive, as most of these women have no formal education. When they are allowed to leave, they are often victims of life-threatening diseases like AIDS, without a place to go. In all probability they will continue in the area and start soliciting and earning independently. Though Lakshmi refuses to entertain a customer who is drunk or reluctant to use a condom, she gets herself checked regularly for sexually transmitted diseases.

What bothers Lakshmi is what will happen of her two sons— Rakesh (11) and Monish (13). Her children aren't aware of her profession and are under the impression that she earns money by working as a maid in the nearby buildings. "I want them to become good individuals and have a good lifestyle, and I don't want them to be involved in anything related to prostitution," says Lakshmi,well aware of the social stigma associated with the red-light area.

Lakshmi has to deal with 15–16 customers a day and earns between Rs 350–1000 from each. Of all the encounters she has had so far, one in particular still haunts her.

"I recall it as a usual day in business. Around 9 pm I was trying to call Mrs Shah and ask her to check on Rakesh and Monish. And suddenly I froze. I can feel his breath at the back of my neck and I shiver. Fear gripped me at my very core. I recognise his breath—he is the *sahib* who gives extra money to my *garhwali* (pimp) to meet me and usually what follows is discordant sex, something that chills me to my bones. He is not kind and usually gets very aggressive and threatens to beat me if I deny him. Before I can turn, his muscled arms grip me. I try to wriggle free, but he slams me against the wall. And suddenly my eyes get a little blurry as blood oozes out of the cut at the side of my head. I slide down against the wall covering my face, my hands soaked in blood. As his buckle is undone, I swallow a gulp. I shut my eyes, hoping for this to get over as fast as possible. His hands grope me, tearing and removing my clothes. These are exactly the times when "why" arises in my mind, asking for a justification for why I chose to be a part of this flesh trade. This is a pathetic world of chauvinistic men who in every way possible want to gain proprietorship of a woman's body!" An indepth study of the red-light area reflects the dehumanising situation that the commercially sexually exploited women face every day. The only hope for these women are the NGOs that have been working to improve their condition. They also try to educate them and help them bring up their children.

Lakshmi says she owes a lot to these NGOs and hopes for a future when life will be different. She gazes up at the sky and softly whispers, "One day, this will change!" Then she smiles, refusing to divulge her identity and asking for anonymity, turns around and walks back to reality.

It's play time

There's a peal of laughter coming from the playground next door. Children are running, skipping and playing together. Some boys are playing cricket on the other side of the ground. The scene is a joyful one. Until it dawned that it was a flashback. That playground was replaced with a mall. There were honking cars and people flocked outside. The city is facing a tremendous space crunch; children are losing out on open-play spaces. Losing parks and playgrounds is considered to be collateral damage in the path of progress. The city gets denser as time passes, migrants keep flowing in, and the need for housing is a pressing issue. In the midst of waves of change, we're losing community spaces. Playgrounds and community spaces aren't always given as much importance as they should. An Austrian architect, Martina Spies noticed this and knowing the importance of play spaces herself, decided to build playgrounds for children.

"I am born and brought up in Austria—one of the most beautiful countries of the world, full of wealth, fresh air and clean water from the Alps. I come from a very open-minded and liberal family and I was always free to choose what I wanted to do as a profession. My father was a builder and politician and he still influences me in the best way of life. He is also part of Anukruti," she said. Anukruti is a non-profit organisation dedicated to making playgrounds and community spaces by creatively using residual spaces in the city.

"I came to Mumbai after my work in Ahmedabad in 2008. I worked in a small office (DCOOP) and made a lot of friends in this charming city. One day I strolled around with a friend and suddenly we stood in the middle of Dharavi. I was so fascinated by the people. It was like a dense huge village in the middle of the megacity of Mumbai. I got curious and wanted to experience it more. After a while, I decided to start my PhD about five different places in Dharavi. I got to know many people there, also many kids. I saw their problems, primarily the lack of space, especially girls in particular. I started to think about it and slowly the idea of Anukruti came to my mind," Martina explains.

"We started Anukruti last year when I finished my research project in Dharavi. I thought people should get something out of it. Research shouldn't happen only on paper! Mary, my dear friend from Dharavi, helped me set it up. She is also a part of Anukruti now. Mary works as a social worker for NIRMAN and helps HIV-positive people and migrants with problems in Dharavi. She helps me find suitable places within Dharavi where we can set up a micro-playground. Also, Sumeet Gade is a friend and supports me a lot. We have already set up a little community centre in Dharavi. Sumeet is very much involved in community work, especially with children. We're trying to set up a little playground in front of the community centre. This will be our next project."

Martina recalls, "As a child, I remember that I played a lot with my friends in the garden and close surroundings, in the fresh air. In

Europe we have so many playgrounds for everyone! When I came to India to work as an architect in 2005 right after my studies at the University of Applied Arts in Vienna, I felt so privileged and I suddenly saw the difference: there were so many kids, especially in urban slums, who don't have the possibility to play. EVERY child should have the right to play and use open and green space as safe and healthy environments.

"I believe that playgrounds and little gathering spaces, especially for women, are important hotspots in a megacity like Mumbai. They can influence people in a very positive way and help to strengthen little neighbourhoods. Children, especially, need space for themselves and it is crucial for a city to provide this for them. I believe that even the smallest leftover spaces are important and should be transformed into playgrounds and gathering spaces. Our new vision is the design of our urban flowers in the sizes small, medium and large. They are platforms and portable playgrounds. An urban flower can be a library, a sitting space, a space to swing and balance, or just a gathering space for women. The community is responsible for it. What's important is that you can lock them at night. We are also trying to transform school courtyards into playgrounds and little libraries. We could also set up an urban flower there. Also, school courtyards are safe spaces.

"Our first playground has been set up in Khar Danda and it is especially made for the children living nearby in the slums. We built it with nearly 100 per cent recycled materials that we got from the city! You need so little money, but a lot of ambition and strength to work on playgrounds in the city. Sometimes I feel it is harder to set up a playground than to build a posh 20-storey building! Our next playground will follow soon. We'll work on the urban flower project soon. We will search for leftover spaces within the city and I'm sure we'll find little pockets. Mumbai faces a lot of problems, but for me it is a warm and fascinating city. People are so friendly and warm hearted and I love the street food! Everything happens in the streets in Mumbai. Why shouldn't children get a safe and joyful part of the city too?" Martina asks.

Anukruti also manufactures handmade leather bags made by the leather workers of Dharavi. Each Anukruti bag is a 100 per cent non-profit product. The money is used to buy materials needed, to pay fair wages to the artisans, and to build modern and safe playgrounds. "During my work in Dharavi I could set up many contacts with leather workers there. So I started to design Anukruti leather bags of the best quality and with a unique design, with the punched dots in the leather and the colourful cotton fabric inside. We started our online shop a couple of months ago and we are already successful in Europe. There are only three to five pieces per design, so it is a very exclusive range of bags. We already financed two playgrounds within the last three months. I'm very happy about it," Martina smiled.

"Half of the year I stay in Mumbai, the other half in Austria. I love the Alps and enjoy it so much. So I enjoy combining these two countries in my life. Austrians are very similar to Indians. We are warm hearted people who enjoy family life. My Indian friends keep visiting me in Austria and my Austrian friends often come here. So it's just perfect. My family loves India and they visit me regularly," she said.

Mujawar's travels

Mazgaon, one of the seven islands that make up Mumbai, is today largely inhabited by the Bohra Muslim community and the Catholics. It offers a lot more than just its architectural skyline—there are ships that are manufactured and repaired, docks that conduct imports and exports, and many such subsidiary commercial activities. Also, there are a number of jetties dotting this coast ferrying people across the bay and along the coast. Many of them are those who travel back and forth to earn a living.

Living and working with the smell of the salty air and raw fish, there is a ferry*wallah* named Amir Mujawar, who operates between Mazgaon and Mumbra. "I was the first among my brothers to come here from Tausaad in Chiplun district, to Bombay. It was a journey by ship from Jaigad Bandar in the year 1984," recalls Mujawar.

His father worked for IK MARINE, while Mujawar spent his childhood fishing along the coastal area. After he completed his ninth grade he decided to leave school so that he could support his family financially.

After travelling to Bombay and wandering for a while, Mujawar reached Ballard Pier, an old business district in the city and home to shipping companies and the headquarters of the Mumbai Port Trust. He got into BPS with the help of people from his village who were employed there and worked at Ranak Bandar for approximately five years. "There were barely three sailing per day, because of which he earned about Rs 400 per month. Because of the low frequency, work seemed very slow and easy. The time we spent waiting to take off could be put to better use," he decided.

Soon he discovered connections with his people that helped him move closer to the prime area of the Gateway of India, where he worked as a ferry*wallah* for about another five years. Watching families, teenagers and eager tourists filled with excitement and joy, Mujawar counted the days to visit his home even as he sailed them safely across the sea to their destinations. "The ship had gradually started becoming another home for me. We would work, eat and sleep together on board."

Working for eight hours daily fetched him Rs 8,000 per month, but his work often saw him skipping *namaaz*; so the search for a new job began again. That's when he found employment at Dockyard Road, which provided him not only with a mosque close by, but also the flexibility of working hours. "I like Dockyard the best, for it has a lot more to offer with its close proximity to my second house, where my family now resides; it helps me to travel smoothly daily. In the course of time I called my brothers here and now we all work together!"

Mujawar got married in 1996 in his village and later brought his family to Bombay. They stay near Antop Hill; his four children study at the municipal school, while his wife works as a maid. Amir earns around Rs 9,000 per month and they manage to run the show together, even after paying a rent of Rs 3,500. "I manage to keep in touch with my mother and relatives; at times my mother stays for a while with all of us, moving between houses we brothers now have, so that we all get to spend time with her!"

In a year he gets only 13 holidays during which he makes it a point to visit his village. He's happy with all he has and doesn't object when he needs to work extra hours to manage to support his family. "At times of financial crisis I may work for 16 hours a day, but with my brothers around now I feel supportive and responsible for all."

He is happy where he is. "I miss spending Ramzan at my village, but I prefer to stay and sail around here with my family. People know me here and I too have started knowing people—it feels good to be known!" Awaiting his own destination, Amir continues to sail people across the sea to theirs.

No laughing matter

As the sun goes down to kiss the horizon, it casts a soft, golden glow over seven men sitting in a row. Regulars at Jogger's Park, these men in their 70s gather every evening at "their" spot on the wall along the sea facing the mangroves and the sunset. They discuss their day-to-day lives, reminisce about bygone days and discuss stocks—a common retirement hobby for all of them. A couple of metres away people of a younger generation jog and walk briskly past.

One of these men is Brijlal Bhatia, who was born and brought up in Kanpur. He graduated from IIT and took up a government job there. A family friend, an industrialist based in Kanjurmarg in Bombay (as it was called then), advised Brijlal to move to the city for its wider range of opportunities and better pay scale.

Brijlal moved to Bombay in 1961 and absolutely hated it. He lived in Kalbadevi in the backroom of his brother-in-law's shop. The crowds, lack of space and inaccessibility of decent housing irked him. Sitting in the small, dark room at night, he was miserable.

He was employed by the Indian Oil Company in 1966, but was keen on working for a government company with offices in other cities, so that he could be transferred. He was hoping to move to either Kanpur or Delhi, where he had family. After several failed applications, Brijlal was finally transferred to Madras (now Chennai). It was not what he had been hoping for, but he was happy to leave Bombay. He spent two years there before being transferred back to the big city he so disliked.

Being several ranks higher in the company by then, Brijlal was allotted a flat in Versova in the Indian Oil Company Colony close to the beach. Soon after, Brijlal met a Bombay girl he fell in love with and married her. He slowly made peace with the city. Having a family and a "home" helped a great deal.

When national banks introduced their first home loan schemes, he decided to buy a flat of his own. He found a sea-facing apartment he liked at Carter Road, Bandra. It was closer to his office in Bandra East, and his wife liked the locality for its schools and other facilities. Buying the flat was a good investment for them as well, with its value having grown a lot since then.

Brijlal's two children are now grown up and well-settled into their own lives and careers. His son, an IT engineer, is a director in a software company and his daughter lives in Delhi, married to a Supreme Court lawyer. "It is gratifying to see my children travel, choose their jobs and live in the city of their choice. Such mobility was something I could only dream of when I was their age," he says.

"Joining the Indian Oil Company was the best decision I could have made. It has given me a comfortable life today." Brijlal explains that the company covered, and still covers, all his hospital bills and gives him a good pension and benefits.

Representing a generation that aspired for the highly regarded "government job" back in the 1960s, Brijlal, now in his golden years, is a satisfied man, investing in the stock market—not so much to make money, but to spend his time productively. Staying fit is a prominent aspect of his life, and its growing importance as he gets older, is not lost on Brijlal. Every morning at 7am he makes his way from his Carter Road flat to Jogger's Park for a daily session of laughter and yoga.

Popular with retired folk, the Jogger's Park Laughter Club is a gathering of about 20–30 people every morning in the triangular garden opposite the main park. Brijlal volunteers as the club's financial advisor.

Started as a laughter club, it drew the health conscious who, in their old age, understood the importance and health benefits of laughter and happiness, an emotion that seems to grow scarce as urban frustration levels rise.

These days, however, they have cut down on the laughter therapy and do more yoga and other morning exercises instead because of complaining neighbours. Brijlal cites the example of a Santa Cruz-based laughter club being taken to court by a residents' association. "We do not want all that trouble here," he says. "The point, after all, is to be happy."

The road less taken

"There are millions of kids who are lining up to be actors even though they don't possess a shred of talent. Sometimes it is better to find your own true calling than to attempt something that isn't your destiny. Sometimes it's better to have an option B," says Krishen Hooda, upcoming filmmaker who is currently in the throes of making his feature length "Rebellious Pyaar".

The aspiring cricketer turned filmmaker knows. "I was originally a resident of Rohtak, Haryana. My father was an army officer and he got posted to Mumbai in 2003. I was interested in cricket and in my head, I played quite well. I was living in the Kalina military camp, and travelled to Santacruz to train at the camp there," says Hooda. Mumbai has a number of cricket training camps from Oval Maidan to the Poddar grounds, all dotted with young cricketers dressed in white at all times of the day, wiping sweat from their brows under the searing hot sun.

Krishen Hooda combines both the passions of Mumbai, Bollywood and cricket. In the city, as all over India, cricket is revered.

Indeed, the erstwhile God of cricket, Sachin Tendulkar, resides in the city.

"But passion, alas, is no match for talent," says Mr Hooda. "I was kicked off the team since the coach thought that I wasn't good enough. I was heartbroken, and I left," only to be steered in the direction of Bollywood, the industry that attracts flocks of newcomers from the far corners of the country. Andheri and Versova are home to hundreds of such aspirants who brave sky-rocketing rents for tiny hovels that they share with many other hopefuls. There are queues outside all the major studios and the coffee shops are filled to bursting with those who hope to be "spotted".

In Mumbai, instead of the producers scouting for suitable leads for their films, a throng of Bollywood "strugglers", as they call themselves, scout for opportunities and any possible role by bombarding studios with photographs and portfolios. Sometimes, in a stroke of luck, they may catch the eye of an influential producer or casting agent in a mall, coffee shop or gym. It is common to see these hopefuls working out in expensive gyms dressed to the nines.

Krishen had it relatively easy in this unforgiving industry. What worked for him was the fact that he handled his initial failures pragmatically. "In 2008 I decided to go to Greenwich University, but my friend Randeep Hooda, who lived in the same locality as me in Haryana, advised me to pursue my passion instead of running behind a degree that would mean nothing to me. So I decided to hang around Prithvi theatre and scout for work." Started by Prithviraj Kapoor, a successful Bollywood actor, the Prithvi theatre runs plays by established theatre actors and the café outside is populated by young hopefuls who believe that in order to learn the intricacies of acting; they must first work in theatre.

In the open-air café it is not uncommon to see these individuals waxing eloquent about the history of theatre or the virtues of an upcoming play over endless cups of coffee. "I worked as a backstage hand. Meanwhile, in my free time I auditioned for bit roles in theatre productions. When none of these tactics worked, I decided to write a play for myself," says Krishen, with the never-say-die attitude of a track runner. Indeed, his first play was called 'Red Track' and was based on the life of an athlete.

"Friends might provide you contacts, but there are no networking circles as such. I was incredibly lucky to have a producer for a friend, who told me that my real skills lay in writing and filmmaking. I took his advice to heart, and hurled myself headfirst into the project," says Hooda. The rest was an uphill track for him, as he directed and wrote four different plays and a slew of movies. His production house was named 'Red Track' after his first play, and that was also one of the first feature length movies he produced.

"There are people who hang on to their dreams with all their might, and who do questionable things to achieve them. I have also been asked to enter into certain deals with filmmakers that would have tarnished my self-respect. However, what ultimately matters is the choices that you make, and the road that you choose," says Hooda. Not everyone has the ability to scale the highest mountain, so maybe the easier route is to take the tunnel through it.

"I remember an incident from my struggling days. One day I spotted Yashwant Singh, an actor who has played prominent roles in movies like Singh is King, and greeted him. He brushed me off with a curt 'hi'. Today the same man is the lead in a film produced and directed by me. It is funny how equations change in this industry,

155

and how one day you are clutching at cards and later handing out the deck," laughs Hooda.

The dynamics of the film industry—the greed, the conceit and the changing equations—might perhaps be the perfect ingredients for a potboiler Bollywood movie. And yet, thousands of aspirants prefer to perform this ritualistic dance in search of fame. Some manage to reach the top of the deck, while most others just clutch the cards and pray for more.

Help for self-help

Soaked in the glorious evening sunlight and drizzling rain, the lush green hills and run-down structures of dairy farms scattered over the landscape, look dramatic from the balcony of Lake View, an apartment in Royal Palms, Goregaon. "In a city like Mumbai, it is almost impossible to find a place so quiet and peaceful like this. On one side we have the hills continuing from Film City, on the other side are the ones from the National Park," says Josef in his accented English, as he walks into his living room and makes himself comfortable. "Initially a part of one of the biggest self-sustained green dairy farm zones—Aarey Milk colony, run by the state government—this land was bought by a private developer when the system started falling apart. While the milk centres are still operating, the fringes of this green lung are being eaten up by development and some displaced leopard's prowl in the area."

A former Swiss national, Josef runs the Child and Family Relief Foundation, an NGO that provides "Free Correctional Treatment" to children suffering from deformities, mostly due to polio. How did a marketing manager from Switzerland decide to enter humanitarian work in India? "In my early twenties, travelling around Southeast Asia, I decided to visit India in 1987. And the first place I visited was Mumbai." Over a cup of coffee Josef continues, "During my initial days I was a victim of a massive culture shock. Mumbai was a total contrast to Switzerland where streets are very clean, the basic sanitary conditions are a must in every house and there are absolutely no slums. Due to the same reason, India tends to be a bad memory for many foreigners, but for me it was mysterious, yet homely. Hence I decided to stay." Inspired by the works of Mother Teresa, Josef decided to contribute in some manner to social activities.

For the first three years, Josef ran a garment export business and alongside, volunteered for few social activities run by his friends. He soon began to learn Hindi which helped him understand the country and its people better. During his social work, Josef came across many people who were suffering from disabilities and deformities due to polio, the country's largest epidemic then. Deeply moved by the life stories and struggles of the disabled poor, Josef and his late wife Verena Suess, who was a fashion designer in Switzerland, started the NGO, Polio Child Relief.

"We travelled across the country undertaking massive polio camps. It was while working jointly with several organisations on a city wide polio-camp in 1997 that we came in contact with Dr P Desai, who was one of the surgeons at the camp," says Josef. In the late 1990s, when polio infections in the country started dropping drastically, PCR decided to broaden services to a wider range of disabilities and to set up a centre in Mumbai where patients in need could be treated. "With an association with Dr Desai we started a new project whose main objective was to improve the lives of the physically disabled by providing access to required facilities,

158

with the help of corrective surgeries, physiotherapy and necessary orthopaedic appliances so that they could walk on their own without assistance. We help for self-help," explains Josef.

Later on, PCR-Mumbai was renamed Child and Family Welfare Foundation. Over time patients started to come to Mumbai for treatment even from rural areas and faraway states. So the project grew on a small and steady basis and individual care of patients was developed, which led to many success stories. "In Mumbai we have a tie-up with a hospital in Malad where Dr Desai and many other specialists treat patients, with out charging any consultation fees," says Josef.

Then a personal crisis hit Josef. His wife Verena fell ill with cancer and passed away. "Even after facing a lot of hurdles, I decided to take the project forward, because it was Verena's solemn wish that the project—dear to her and in which she worked humbly and enthusiastically—should continue at any cost," says Josef.

"Many a times while offering help people have asked me: what is in it for you? Well, I would say the smile on their face is the best reward. Once, as a part of one of our projects, we took the inmates of Mankhurd Mental hospital for a picnic to Aksa beach. I have never seen such happy people in my life. The sight of them playing and enjoying was too overwhelming. There are many other such stories that are keeping us going, I remember a girl who used to crawl due to a shortness of her limbs. She got a limb-lengthening surgery done and is currently working as a nurse. One main lesson that I've learned during my services is that when someone receives help for their disability, their self-esteem often takes a leap upward. If that is achieved, then we say that our treatment is completely successful," he smiles.

During the course of his stay in Mumbai, Josef has seen Mumbai grow. In the initial days, the itinerary for their project was available only in town. But in the last few years the suburbs developed drastically with the emergence of fast communication and land availability. "I have stayed in many parts of Mumbai, Powai, Peddar Road, Versova, Chembur, etc. Along with all the good friends and great memories, Mumbai has also given me bothersome asthma, for the past 10 years, which was the main reason I shifted to Aarey colony even before this area was much developed. But now the asthma has gotten worse and my doctor suggests I relocate to a less polluted area," he adds. Even after trying to stay in the city, Josef has now run out of options and hence, as his doctor suggested, is planning to move to Nasik.

Recently Josef married again; his wife, Nisha, was from a small village in West Bengal. "Even though I have lived in India for 30 years now, another aspect of this country has opened up for me. The experiences of staying in Nisha's village are very interesting and different. It put me more in touch with the life of an 'aam aadmi'. That is when I realise afresh that, it doesn't matter how long you stay here, there are always new experiences on your way," he believes. Had he first visited another city first, would he have still chosen to settle down in India? He says, "I think NO, I wouldn't. Visiting Mumbai was like following my destiny and as soon as I reached here, I felt I was home. Now I proudly call myself a Mumbaikar!"

Carving a niche

"Mumbai's reputation preceded it for me in my hometown in Uttar Pradesh. They told me this was the greatest city in India, and business would be ideal here. I came here seven years ago, and look at it! This is our greatest city." said Dilshad Abid Dastangrins, beckoning me to his shop.

It's June and 5 o' clock in the evening, raining cats and dogs. Dilshad can hardly be heard over the battering of a typical Mumbai downpour on the weak asbestos providing a cover to his shop, filled with ornately carved mirror frames, shrines, panels and uncut wood stacked in corners. Crouched on the floor of his shop with a toupee on his head and a chisel in his hand, Dilshad is busy carving an intricate peacock motif over a half-done wooden shrine.

"Most of us here in this line of woodcarving shops are from Saharanpur, 20–30 years old; young hands work faster. Also, it's not a family business. It is more like an extension of the Saharanpur woodcarving community," he says, indicating the long row of shops on the pavement bordering the busy thorough fare of Swami Vivekananda Road, one of the main arteries between Bandra and Mahim.

Around us wander goats with watermelon skins in their jaws, street kids play in puddles formed under the shiny silver skywalk built by MMRDA to direct railway commuters, now shelter to many homeless, and the peevish traffic honks nosily.

"Our town is famous for its wood-carving industry, which is more than 300 years old some say, I am uncertain though," says Dilshad about his village located between New Delhi and Dehradun near the foothills of the Himalayas. "However, woodcarving is now no longer community driven. My father was a farmer. I was inspired by my friends around me who were in this business and were able to make something so beautiful."

He continues, "My family still continues farming. We grow fruits, grains and other things like *basmati* rice, mangoes, cotton, sugarcane and tobacco. Though our lands are very fertile with the streams and rivers from the Himalayas, it is a very nature oriented existence, hence there is a lot of uncertainty. So I moved to Mumbai with them for more opportunity. My family lives at Saharanpur, so do most of the others."

Much like his fellow immigrants, Dilshad believes in using the city as a commercial base. Living simple, frugal lives here, often resorting to 10 to 15 people sharing a small space in the nearby slum; their hard-earned money is used to buy land, tractors and animals, or to build *pukka* homes back home. An admirable feat, considering many were paid labourers on farms of landlords till a few years ago.

"I stay here in Mumbai for usually two months of work, and then go back there. But I've been in the city for the last six months because business has blossomed. There are a few more customers than last year." He shrugs, "I don't know details. It's a 12-hour stay-in-the-shop job. I stay in the shop the whole day, and just go home to sleep. What else can I do in the city? Joy ride on these open trains? I work hard here for a few months, then return to the north and enjoy life in my village."

Though most of shops have similar products "there are no competitive brawls among us. No one lowers their prices to admit better interest from customers. It's our individual work that talks," explains Dilshad. "This small shrine goes for Rs 5,000, and these smaller mirror-frames go for Rs 500; the biggest, an ornate oval six-foot mirror frame with thickly embossed roses in its wooden whorls over there will go for Rs 20,000."

However, they have to endure long waiting periods. "Customers are irregular. It's such a business! However, in our free time we take care of each other's shops, we comment and gossip about our neighbours and co-tenants, or the vagaries of SV Road. It's like being a part of a brotherhood of Saharanpur. Often when we want to send money home, one of the men who is travelling home takes our share to be given to our family, and we pay him extra for that." Why not use a banking system? He shrugs. Another detail Dilshad is unaware of.

It's the sound of the *azan* that concludes the conversation. Dilshad shuffles off for *namaaz* at the huge green mosque that defines the Muslim community here.

163

Married to the city

"It has been over 25 years now," she laments."Mumbai never really felt like home to me. I miss the hoopla around Durga puja, the *adda* with like-minded friends and the curious chatter and buzz that emanates from houses on sleepy afternoons in Calcutta," she reminisces.

Indian marriages follow a tradition that involves men bringing home brides from their native place after an "arranged" marriage. Dozens of prospective suitors are sifted through in a process that involves judging a person by their qualifications and physical attributes. "Arranging" a marriage involves the parents of both parties giving their approval. At times, this is all that is needed; the future couple's opinions play no role in the matter.

It was after this process that she arrived in the city of Mumbai like dozens of other brides wrenched from their hometowns to be life partners of men they did not know. And like weary strangers they approach both their marriage and the city with hesitation and fear.

"My parents were originally from Bangladesh, but were

forced to immigrate to Calcutta when the war broke out. As a child, I always thought of my mother as a misfit, an alien to the highbrow life of Calcutta society." She kneads dough for *luchis*, her *shaakha pola* clinking together in tandem with her thoughts. Outside, through the pigeon wire-meshed window, the sun sets over a balmy suburban cityscape." Eventually I was married to a man from Mumbai with high educational qualifications, but not before I had fallen in love with the culture and poetry of Calcutta. It became difficult for me to imagine a life outside the confines of the four walls of my house. I was exhilarated and frightened at the possibility of a life with a progressive man in a progressive society. I had lived a sheltered life till then, with fixed schedules and a prescribed set of duties for daughters. And to be honest, I packed those qualities into my baggage when I was preparing for the journey to Mumbai."

So when she arrived, "I was in for a culture shock." She smiles as she relives the memories of those days." I didn't know the language; the rude ways of the locals shocked me. For the first time in my life I was truly experiencing a cosmopolitan society. There were Maharashtrians living next door, and Gujaratis living on the floor above. They all came from different backgrounds, but they had lived in and survived this city, and that gave me the strength to slowly acknowledge the pulse of Mumbai, to tap its rhythm and accustom myself to its rules. With time, I learnt to bargain with grocers who refused to bring the produce up to our door, but spread their mats next to the open gutters and hawked their wares."

Her life is a series of such anecdotes, some of which she chuckles over. "It was right after my marriage that I set out on an errand. I did not speak a word of Hindi. After clubbing together a few words I managed to wring out a sentence roughly translating to 'give me a dozen eggs'. But my accent was so thick that no matter how much I tried to pronounce the word 'baida' (eggs), it came out as 'kanda' (onions). It was the day that I walked a couple of kilometres only to be offered onions instead of eggs!"

After almost 25 years in the city, she still mispronounces simple words and remains befuddled by certain phrases that are a part of the city's lingo. A few years into her marriage, a colleague dropped by; as he got up to leave, he used the oft-repeated phrase 'Chalo, chalte hain!' or "Come, let's go!' or 'See you later!'. Unaware of the idiom, she got up to leave with her guests, only to be greeted by peals of laughter.

The city can be unforgiving of those who are not accustomed to its cruel ways. Yet she managed to stick it out through sheer adaptability and strength. She has two daughters, both true citizens of Mumbai. They cannot speak Bengali well, and refuse to accompany her to Calcutta. "I have to get out of Mumbai every year. I have to breathe. I may have been married into one city, but I have given my heart to another."

She spends her free time at the Ramakrishna Mission with other Bengali women in the city. They reminisce about their childhoods spent in the peeling bungalows of Calcutta, share their general disdain of the *Mumbaiyya* ways, and organise meets and prayer sessions. Her quintessentially suburban house is embellished with reminders of her history. A Bengali calendar hangs next to the Catholic calendar and the copper urns used by her late father find a special space in her loft. Every nook and corner holds her possessions and has been personalised by her.

Her cupboard is home to a handwoven doll made of traditional Bengali textiles, her keychain displays a picture of the famous Kalighat in Calcutta.

Every day people come to Mumbai and make it their home, some of their own free will, others grudgingly. Some, like her, arrive as reluctant brides. Each has a special story to tell, some with love and affection, others with tolerance and a few, with dislike and hate.

The wordsmith

"If you get into a BPO and are not one of those quick-money types, you're probably going to get addicted to the place. You'll never come out. It's that vast." Jeremy, dressed in a dark blue rapper-cap, a mauve polo-shirt and knee-length blue denim shorts explains, walking towards a swath of open, undeveloped land on the south-east of the nearby estuary. Over it all, looms a battalion of huge, minimalistic, cuboidal dark-tinted glass buildings that employ half of the various BPO (Business Process Outsourcing) businesses in Mumbai.

"There are so many opportunities there that I've known people who've been there since the beginning, 10 years ago. It's like a little self-sufficient world with a nascent edgy, fast-paced culture that is vulnerable to nepotism and general skulduggery on one side, and on the good side, personality-development, people skills and official progress for kids with small academic resumés. It's a fast-changing rank hierarchy and there are a variety of jobs you can earn if you play your cards right. You have to be smart. It's a great opportunity for youngsters to dig their heels in and do some honest work."

He says this as if to emphasise how misunderstood the job is,

169

in indignant comment against the general opinion that BPOs are hubs for drop-outs to make quick cash, snowballing into a hedonistic yuppie culture. In the early 2000s, many international telecommunications companies like Hutchinson 3G set up call centres in Mumbai to employ thousands to regulate a huge volume of customer service calls. It was a cheap labour option.

The job requires employees to deal with the various customer-service-related problems over the phone, with one small catch: the customers are a thousand accents away in the English-speaking continents of Europe and Australia.

"I got into the Sales department of Hutch 3G when I was 19, after passing my secondary education in the HSC board, while I simultaneously did my degree, affiliated to the Mumbai University, from home. After being accepted, you are supposed to undergo a voice and accent training programme, as well as a process programme in which they teach you the policies and techniques of making sales on the phone, since most of us are attuned only to Indian-accented English and have been equipped to memorise textbooks to keep abreast of the world. Once you start it's all about putting in the nine-hour shifts and keeping up the numbers and, crucially not losing customer-salesman etiquette."

"Once, a colleague, a guy, pressurised after a day of zero-successful calls in the Sales Department, lost his temper when an Irish customer rudely rebuffed him on the phone, giving the foul-mouthed Irishman back in kind, in front of the whole call-bay. He was promptly fired our bosses paid special attention to the number of successful calls one made in a day. If you didn't keep high numbers they would mark you and look down on you. If it got worse, they'd send a quietly sinister message for you to come to their cabin and then, while you were alone with them, they'd *bad-cop-good-cop* you, profanities and all."

Jeremy explains that the hierarchy within the organisation is split into many departments: the Sales Department is an outbound service; one has to call the customer. The Retention Department is an inbound service, where the customer who's trying to terminate services has to be offered sugar-coated deals to try to retain him/her. The Collections Department is again outbound, where the absconding customer has to be coaxed to pay pending bills immediately.

"They want brutal efficiency, and they have a whole system designed for it. If a call goes more than three minutes, it's a waste of your (and their) time. You have to utilise your time to get at least 50 successful calls out of 300 in a nine-hour shift," says Jeremy. "It's one reason why I think the movie *The Wolf of Wall Street* was such a hit here. That scene, where Leo outflanks the investor on the phone. A lot of these call-centre guys respect that stuff, because that's what it takes to be successful: guts, guile and consistency, and not everyone has it."

To decompress after a long stint at work, the best cure for the aural malaise is usually an eclectic mix of the best music in the dubstep, trance and house genres. Jeremy is particularly connoisseur-like about his music. An Armin Van Buuren concert band decorates his wrist. He tells me that the lyric-less, repetitive, instrumental quality of the music is synonymous with a focused catharsis, something that wishy-washy pop lyrics usually interrupt. He wears his heart on his sleeve, literally. And a Manchester United pendant around his neck. Not that Jeremy was particularly good at football. "I can't kick a ball straight, neither can I play FIFA. It's started off as a social thing. I tried enjoying it because my friends did. It's that kind of a cultivated passion."

He studied at St Andrew's in Bandra. "I did my BCom and since some of my friends and my sister were in BPOs, I decided to pursue it too," says Jeremy. "The company forever changed the way I deal with people. I am now much wiser, cautious as to who my real friends are, and smarter when it comes to pleasing my superiors." To him, the experimental culture of his past was in fact a stepping stone rather than a stumbling block to success for a man who had to make the most of his academic shortcomings. Success for him is seen in the new family man that he is: in 2010 he married Alokita, a co-worker, and after three years they had a daughter. It was certainly a move in a different direction, one that was a far cry from late-night pot-smoking sessions, alcohol binges and nicotine stains. The only vestiges of this youth are apparent in the form of his put-on American accent that emerges in formal situations.

This socio-economic global phenomenon of business outsourcing has certainly exposed the financially and technically-segregated youth of the suburbs to foreign culture and opportunities, but the labour here is mono-dimensional in its call format. That's one reason why Jeremy eventually got bored with his job and left for a Japanese transcription firm called Eigo Experts (Japanese for "English") in 2010.

Now he relays subtitled Japanese audio files into English text and sends them to Eigo's clients. The workman-like virtuosity of the Japanese inspires him, and he seriously contemplates the what-ifs of a life that could have allayed some of his academic-shortcomings. "They are so conscientious and dedicated to their professions. The ethic they maintain is staggering. If only I was brought up in their culture. I could have been an artist in many, many things."

The fleeting resident

Shopping for an art project at the Cheap Jack store on Hill Road, her face glows as she browses through the bric-a-brac and crafts, searching for the right type of buttons, thread and fabric paint. Her mauve floral cotton shirt complements her friendly demeanour as it falls over her baby bump. Inspired by the vibrancy of the city, she is embarking on personal creative projects to do while in Mumbai.

Christel Agnes is an artist and graphic designer from Marseille, France. Her husband works for a French multinational company that posted him in Mumbai a year ago on a three-year contract. Christel moved to Mumbai just a month ago and plans to stay on in the city for a year after having her baby.

"I want to be with my husband and support him while he works in India, but it's not easy to quit my job in Europe. I love my work, and it was very difficult for me to get the job that I have there! I am using my maternal leave and taking a year-long sabbatical to be here in India. Health care in Mumbai is good and I have access to domestic help that I would not have been able to afford back in France."

Christel, who is seven months along now, spends her time painting, exploring the city and meeting fellow expatriates and their families. "It's a lively community of expats here in this city," she says. "There are 'Expat Night' parties, French food events and even a special expatriate magazine on Indian culture. For someone who is new to this city, I feel very welcomed by both expats and Indians! Everyone has been warm and friendly."

Still in the honeymoon phase of her move to Mumbai, Christel is fascinated by the city and loves every bit of it. Her husband, who has been here for longer, has a slightly different perspective. Travelling every day from their home in Pali Hill to his office in Powai, he is now beginning to feel the stress of urban life in India, despite all the comforts provided by his company to help him live a life as close to the one he had in Marseille.

With the company providing him a house and chauffeur-driven car, paying the bills and giving him other perks and allowances, it makes a lot of sense, financially, for him to work in Mumbai, even though it meant being away from Christel for a while. For someone who loves travelling and engaging with different cultures, living in Mumbai has been a colourful experience for him. Right from the outset, the house hunt took a whole month, during which time he looked at almost 100 apartments before he finally settled on the one at Pali Hill, which he chose mainly for its location. What he wasn't prepared for, however, were the prolonged negotiations that followed between the flat owner and his company's relocation department. The idea of paying part of the rent in cash to avail tax reductions—a standard practice for a large section of renting Mumbaikars—was completely absurd to him.

Apart from standard Indianisms and head-bobbling, the couple is amazed at the frequency with which household appliances break down and Internet issues arise. On the other hand, they are equally amazed by the round-the-clock availability of repair and maintenance services that, for a price, they can avail of at odd hours and at short notice. Back in France, things work more reliably and such glitches are rare occurrences, but repair services are available only during fixed working hours, which is inconvenient for working families. In India, things like that are flexible.

While urban Indians take the accessibility of house help and the country's large human resource for granted, Christel is yet to grow accustomed to having a maid to help her around the house and run errands. "It's a bit strange, in a nice way, after coming from a place where I had to do all the housework myself," she says. "I think some of the expats here are getting so used to being looked after and pampered, it is going to be very hard for them to return to Europe after this!"

Addicted

"Mumbai somehow is the most random place in the world. The city is maddening if you don't know what to look for," says Namrata Khandelwal. "Amidst the chaos the city still seems to follow a natural rhythm," she states.

"You only realise the importance of something after it's no longer there." Namrata is a third-year student studying dentistry in the educational hub of the country, Kota. "The idea of being in a new city all alone was a haunting thought at the start. I had a nervous breakdown on the very first day in my hostel. I cried myself to sleep that day," she says sheepishly.

Wearing a white cotton *kurta* and her patent lab coat, her distinct brown eyes enhanced with black *kohl*, she is dressed for her first lecture of the day. But before it starts she heads towards the college mess and picking at the white slurry which is supposed to be upma, she says, "Beyond anything I miss the food of Mumbai.From the luxurious five-star hotels to the *vada pav* vendor just around every corner, you can satiate your hunger almost anywhere, at any time."

Mumbai would be incomplete without the street food that is the most accessible item on the road, in trains and at almost every corner. Be it in the corporate jungle or on a sidewalk of the busiest street, you will still find places to eat. That is unlike the scenario in Kota, which lacks the cultural mix of Mumbai and is mainly a Gujarati-and Marwari-dominated community, along with many students from various backgrounds and various parts of the country and the world.

"My grandfather came to Mumbai in the early 1950s from Jaipur; my father was born at a government hospital in Kalbadevi," she says. Having grown up in Mumbai for the 19 odd years of her life, going to a new city for further education was a shocking change for Namrata. Hostel life in a small 12 by 12 foot room was a far cry from the luxury and security of her house in the suburbs of Mumbai. "Hostel life teaches you many things, but one in particular, adjustment. You learn to adjust to people around you, the culture around you, the food around you, the place around you," Namrata says proudly.

Over the three years of her course she has finally managed to learn how to do her laundry, cook and keep her room clean, as well as attend lectures and score good marks. "My mother was so proud of me the first time she came to visit me at my hostel. Looking at my tidy little room she even joked, 'Namma, your room was never this clean back in Mumbai!'," laughs Namrata.

"I don't remember how and when I fell in love with Mumbai, but I did. The strong affection I have for the city intensified after I left for Kota. Kota was a totally new city for me, but I made new memories here I can't ever forget. But love for Kota is merely for the amazing places I got to visit, the freedom I got, the responsibility I undertook and the friendships that I fostered which will stay forever," she says with happiness.

Mumbai is an enigma in itself, a city like no other. Even while walking down the streets alone there is a sense of having company that the city projects. "Every time I get back to Mumbai during my study break I only end up eating all the scrumptious food that I am otherwise deprived of throughout the year," says Namrata. "Every time I leave to go back to Kota I am left with a void; it feels like I have left a piece behind me. I am never completely there, I am constantly comparing every aspect of my life in Kota with Mumbai."

Cultural norms in Kota are different. A girl and boy cannot be seen together freely, hugging in public is frowned on and the freedom to wear western clothes is limited. But the tone and the admiration with which folks in Kota talk about Mumbai is special. "Every time I tell someone that I am from Mumbai, you can see a twinkle in their eyes and awe with which they regard me. Many even ask, Have you met Amitabh Bachchan?" says an amused Namrata.

This isn't too shocking, as for most non-residents Mumbai is still regarded as the city of dreams and a factory that makes Bollywood stars. Like so many others, Namrata is enchanted and addicted to the city of her origin: "I am looking forward to Diwali; that is when I will have this semester's study leave and I get to be in my city. Two years are left before I become Dr Namrata Khandelwal and can return to Mumbai and set up my own small clinic," she says grinning happily.

From mills to the sky

In a city of aspiration, hopes and heartbreaks centred on people there exists a structure built exclusively for the pigeons of the city. Now a prominent landmark, Kabutarkhana is a diorama of a streetscape crowded to the brim with scurrying people, honking vehicles, impatient drivers and numerous hawkers. Hundreds of pigeons flying and feeding in the circle built at the centre of the street make the picture come to life.

In front of this circle, next to an ornate Jain temple is Indresh Singh's grain stall which supplies grain to those who come to feed the pigeons of Kabutarkhana. The stall comprises a plank of wood acting as a table to hold heavy bags of grain, a small foldable chair and a parasol. The small scale of the shop aids its staff in packing everything up in a jiffy and fleeing when the BMC vans come to clear the roads of hawkers.

"My grandfather came to Mumbai from Varanasi to earn a living for his family back in Uttar Pradesh. Like other inhabitants of the city, both migrants and natives, he gained employment in the mills of Mumbai. He worked at the textile mills from 1940, till his death in 1955...." Indresh says as his mind wanders to the past.

The cotton mill industry in India was established by urban traders in Mumbai and Ahmedabad and provided employment to millions of workers from all over the country. The textile mill economy reached its zenith at the turn of the 19th century, when it rose to become one of the world's largest industries.

The late 1960s witnessed the downfall of the textile mills.

"My father and uncles came to Mumbai when my grandfather died. They worked at the mill my grandfather worked in, in the same department." Indresh recounts the downfall of the textile mills industry in the late 1960s, "My father was a part of the mill workers' strike. It went on for nearly two years. That's when the Mill Owners Association started to shut the mills down. My father and uncles were unemployed and faced the debilitating pressure of survival and lack of livelihood to feed our families."

The textile industry strike in Mumbai had lasting repercussions on the city and its residents. The aftermath can be seen in the lives of former mill workers, their children and also the social structure of the city. On 18 January 1982, one of India's largest strikes began under the leadership of Datta Samant to increase the workers' wages. "Due to worsening financial conditions and dwindling hopes of receiving any compensation, my father and his brothers decided to sell their small house in a chawl near Siddhivinayak *mandir*. My uncles moved to different parts of the city, wherever they could find cheaper accommodation. My father decided to stay back at Dadar."

The already declining industry coupled with the long strike led mill owners to move their plants to more favourable locations, leaving the lives of millions of mill workers irreparably shattered.

Some survived the ordeal; others were engulfed by poverty and decrepitude. Making ends meet was the hardest challenge for the unemployed workers.

"Like many others, my father too fell into the clutches of poverty. After all, he'd been a part of the movement for nearly two years without any income. There came a point in our life when we didn't have food to eat. That was when we hit rock bottom," Indresh said gravely. At that time children had to drop out of school because their fathers had lost their jobs. People lost their houses along with their income. Hopes were smashed and futures looked bleak as the unemployed men tried to dabble in other professions to sustain their families. Several worked as contract workers without pension or benefits. Crime spread through the streets of Mumbai carrying the pain and desperation of the strike to unparalleled heights.

"Despite the conditions of society, my father chose not to get involved in criminal activities and started this business. He opened a stall here in Kabutarkhana and our financial condition gradually improved. When I grew up I decided to continue with this business. At this point, there's so much competition outside. Starting a new business seemed pointless to me, so I decided to continue what my father started. We've been in this business for 32 years now. My father became a part of this city when he came here. I was born and brought up in this city. It is a part of me, like I'm a part of it. I've studied here, I started my family here. I don't feel like an outsider. I've kept my grandfather and father's IDs of the time when they worked at the mill. The mills and the strike are a part of my life, like they're a part of the city. They wounded us the way it wounded the city." Indresh looks at the bags of grain beside him. The textile mill industry strike changed the face of Mumbai forever with a painful twist in its tale. It changed the fate of everyone involved. It shaped our growth. It shaped Mumbai's history.

"The only possible regret I have is not having taken a licence for our shop when I could have. We have to flee every time the BMC vans come. For them, we're encroaching on public space. Nowadays people are protesting against our business; they believe that pigeons spread disease and they shouldn't be fed. It is a matter of belief. Jain devotees feed these pigeons because it's a religious act, much like Hindus feed cows. The people who come to my stall are not just Gujarati and Marwari people. At least 30 per cent of people who buy grain from me are Maharashtrians. Everyone feeds pigeons. Two in a hundred people in this city really object to feeding pigeons. This doesn't affect my business much. We go on with our work, regardless of what people think." Indresh is firm.

Kabutarkhana is surrounded by a Jain temple, a Hanuman temple, a mosque and a church and is considered a holy spot or a melting pot of religions meeting here. The birds become a kind of focal point.

"We come here at six in the morning when the pigeons come and we leave at six in the evening when they go." Indresh watches the flying pigeons. Unknowingly, his life has been shaped by the lives of these birds. Their timings have become his.

Their relationship is one that goes beyond business, something that is both intangible and intimate. He smiles, "We're treading at our own comfortable pace now. I don't see any hurdle in the immediate future, definitely not what my father and his brothers saw in the 1980s." He rests his back against a tree, sitting on a small concrete seat on the sidewalk in the shade of the Jain temple. His employee fills a tin with grain and sells it to someone who wants to feed the pigeons in Kabutarkhana, just like so many others who come and go every day.

Old is gold!

It is one of the oldest bazaars in South Mumbai and it has effectively reflected the changing ways of the city over a span of 150 years. Chor Bazaar (thieves' market), initially named 'Shor Bazaar' (noisy market) until it was mispronounced by the British, is nothing less than a popular antique itself!

They say, "If you lose something in Mumbai, you can buy it back at Chor Bazaar." As the name suggests the market was once said to be home to many stolen goods. "You develop a good eye along with experience that helps you distinguish between the real and the fake," says Salim, who has owned a shop here for the last 35 years.

Salim came with his chacha from Jamnagar to spend his vacations helping with his work. His chacha was a paan masala seller and Salim would often help him collect supplies. He grew up in Jamnagar with his two brothers under the discipline of his father, who was an ayurvedic doctor, and his softer mother.

"Being the first one to step out of home to earn my living, it wasn't that difficult; my chacha supported me morally and helped start the business by 1983." Salim got married in1980 in Jamnagar; by this time he had already seen partitions in the family over the past few years, so he decided to take control of his life and ambitions.

"In those days, travelling from Jamnagar to Mumbai would be a 24-hour-long journey unlike today's 16-hour trip. Joint families have now started becoming nuclear ones," says Salim. He believes that anyone can get the best from Mumbai, "the richest city", by balancing work and time, key factors to earning a living.

"Shukravaar bazaar (Friday market) is the best time to visit Chor Bazaar." Chor Bazaar can give you anything you need, from vintage goods, art and crafts, furniture and glass lamps to posters of old Bollywood movies, a wide range of paintings and even electronics and automobile spare parts!

"Our customers consist of the common man on one side and the foreign tourist on the other." Being almost a museum of varied artefacts, a shopper must master the art of bargaining before becoming carried away by the urge to buy. Salim finds that "With the value of the Rupee dropping gradually, the cost of rare antique goods has jumped up drastically. The smaller the antique, the greater its value!"

Salim explains that "Other than our regular sources, we also go to different places to purchase different varieties of specialities, even to the Mapusa bazaar at Goa! Trust plays a very important role in our business—we have a few trustworthy sources rather than a variety of them, which helps new customers become fixed customers!" Many sellers and shopkeepers here can manipulate the story of the "duplicate antique" or quote names of well-known artists while selling paintings to reap the benefit from gullible customers, but Salim is one of a kind as he still follows rules set by his principles and morals.

A kind of unusual social worker, Salim helps cure people of kidney stones with the Ayurvedic formula his father passed on to him; some of his patients are treated free of cost. Salim happily accepts sweets in place of money and continues to help people with all he has gained from the traditions handed down by his parents.

Ups and downs

Tucked away in one of the old Todi Mill buildings, Blue Frog is one of Mumbai's best night-spots for music and to catch a live gig. The new-age and plush interiors crowding up with young people on a Friday night are in stark contrast to the defunct textile mill it is housed within. The electronic music with its hints of blues, jazz and South Asian influences is soulful and refreshingly different from the generic EDM that plagues almost every other nightclub in the city. Standing behind her computer and keyboard at the DJ console, Sanaya Ardeshir belts out the indie beats of her music project 'Sandunes'. Like her music, Sanaya does not conform to stereotypes —a friendly, warm and grounded person, she is immersed in her music while working. She does not care for glamour or the limelight, preferring her music to take centrestage.

Sanaya grew up in Pune, where at a young age she began her musical journey by learning to play the piano and keyboards. After Sanaya completed her tenth standard, her father got a job transfer to Mumbai and the whole family moved to the city, settling into a house in South Bombay. Sanaya joined St Xavier's junior college for

Arts, where she made plenty of friends. "Although I was new to the city, I didn't really feel like an outsider. I felt well assimilated because my parents had lived in Bombay before. At college too everybody wanted to meet new people and make friends—everyone was new and many didn't know one other—it was even ground for everyone," she explains. After five years, Sanaya left for London for a higher education in music production. Coincidently, her parents also left the city that same year.

When she decided to move back from London to Mumbai for good, it was different. "This time when I moved back to Bombay, I moved back as an outsider. Life as I knew it earlier was now completely different. My friends had all moved on with their lives and careers and I could not afford to live in South Bombay," says Sanaya. Coping with living costs in Bandra, where she currently lives, has been a quite a challenge for her.

"I had to deal with a lot of the city's civic trials; it's not easy to live here on your own. Civic sense is a bit low, things are not efficient and to top that, it is a very expensive city to live in. I had never experienced these challenges while living under my parents' roof. Suddenly I had to pay all my bills, spend money finding a place to live and figure out what the best area to live in was, while working out a steady-enough source of revenue. However, I think I got quite lucky.

"When I came back to India, I could have moved to any city. It could have been Bangalore, where my parents then lived, or Pune, where I had lived before, or Delhi. I had an open choice. But I specifically chose Bombay because of the wealth of opportunity that was here within the space of work that I am involved in and also because the dregs of my network were here. This was where

I had lived for my last five years in India and I knew a few people involved in the kind of work I wanted to get into. That worked in my favour," Sanaya says. "I started getting work through friends almost immediately. I wanted to do ad jingles and I knew I could not do it anywhere else, since the media industry is based in this city."

She struggled for a while. "I still cannot say that I am out of the woods yet, but it has proved very beneficial for me to socialise within the circles that I do in this city, because that's where all of the work that I do comes from." Mumbai is the crucible of India's music scene, with the best work opportunities for a young music producer of experimental, underground genres. "I will milk Bombay for as long as I can, but as soon as I am able to cut ties I will leave the city, because it is as exasperating as it is rewarding," says Sanaya.

Mumbai audiences are opening up to newer genres and experimental types of music, while the Internet presents an increasingly wide array of choices for the city's growing appetite for eclectic sounds. "We didn't grow up having a deep-rooted music culture because in India what we were fed by the accessible media was Bollywood, pop, hip-hop and now commercial EDM on television. But today people are consuming music differently. It has become "trendy" to be in the know of alternative and underground sub-genres. Back in college, there weren't many people with whom I could talk about music, but now that has changed with these less commercial music scenes getting bigger and drawing larger audiences," says Sanaya. "It will be interesting to see how much this will grow in the coming years, and how much of the music quality will be retained."

With Sandune's fame rising, Sanaya has her gig calendar full,

189

ranging from EP launches to opening acts for international artistes, gigs in other cities and music festivals, with magazine interviews and music video production work squeezed in for good measure. As her career rides atop the crest of a metaphorical sand dune that is life in Mumbai, the civic amenities and social ethics of the city leave much wanting.

It's so not Bollywood!

"They called me Mongrel-san."

"Who all did?"

"My Japanese friends in music school in Carolina. I found it cute."

"You didn't find it offensive?"

He grins. "Maybe at first, but then you get where they're coming from and you even like it. I felt unique. Exotic even." He seems to be amused by his thought.

We're under the double-pitched roof of the True Music School near Lower Parel train station, sitting in the enormous cafeteria. Beautiful cut-outs of the blue sky are visible through the huge skylights in the roof. The interiors are stark white, like a rich modern oasis in the middle of the shabby piecemeal of the slum near the station. Colourful bean bags lie strewn about, on the vivid carpets in the sit-out area and bright artwork on the walls enhance the white starkness. A mezzanine floor peeks out above the wooden stairway.

The True Music School is an educational venture created by established musicians—International and Indian—aimed at people in Mumbai who want to learn music on a professional level. It houses state-of-the-art equipment and sound-proof rooms with security cameras, including a small air-conditioned auditorium, all seamlessly inserted into a formerly dilapidated building.

The auditorium was where the fortnightly "Masterclass" was being held in the evening. Today's Masterclass was a two-hour-long performance session hosted by Pahan. It was themed on a pioneer of the Beatnik jazz movement of the 1960s: John Coltrane. Pahan played saxophone and soprano. His buddy Jimmy was the guitarist. The quintet included a German drummer, a French cellist and an Indian pianist.

Pahan is Nepalese-American. His father was a musician from North Carolina and his mother met his father on one of his forays into the Indian subcontinent as a troubadour. "My dad was travelling the world with his band. A kind of spiritual quest, if you will. And he was at one of these restaurants in Nepal and they started jamming because they had a stage area. After the show, which went on after dinner, my dad met my mom and they started a conversation on Hinduism and music. They talked for three hours straight. She invited him home the next day to meet her family for dinner. Just like that. My dad came. They married a year later."

So why Mumbai?

"I came here to Mumbai two years ago. I was looking for places to teach overseas and I found out about this project through my father's contacts—The True Music School project. It seemed the perfect environment to teach in, because it seemed like a new establishment with a lot of flexibility, and teaching in a high-end American school would have been like a straitjacket. It had been a decade since I last came here and I'd gone to Nepal mostly, only

192

visiting Mumbai for a day. And I never thought of living here. It was all so undeveloped then. So I decided to take the gig, with all the wealth of knowledge I had earned at Carolina, and come here open to the Indian way of things."

So did you like the Indian way?

"As expected, I came here, to Mumbai, expecting a lot from the crowd. And it was exactly as they had said: brutal and beautiful. There is a lack of punctuality here that's so funny. Then there's no consistency in the traffic. There's the endless energy of the street that's not helped by the heat, and yet that's what drives it, I guess. And then there are these multi-talented youngsters who balance professional degrees along with this musical thing. They're doing massive scientific degrees and simultaneously going insane on the piano. I think this building itself epitomises it. Brutal on the outside, but beneath the surface you're just amazed that it could be so… beautiful. I can say the same thing about Blue Frog."

Blue Frog is a music performance hall, a ten minute walk away. Most city musicians use it as a hotspot for their gigs. Peculiarly, it is also inserted into a disused industrial compound warehouse, with sleek acoustical interiors.

The Masterclass is a free event. People are invited by word of mouth and are treated to an acoustically-perfect experience in the small auditorium. Pahan and his quintet played with a spiritual passion. As sweat glistened on his face, his eyes were closed in sacred joy. It is purely the music that has brought him here.

"I was heavily influenced by my dad. He was from North Carolina. And that was the home of so many famous jazz musicians, as I explained today in the auditorium. So jazz has always been my style of music. When I came here, I realised that the trappings of that spirit exist even here, in this other side of the world. Knowing that makes me try even harder at spreading the gospel of John Coltrane." He grins.

A thin French-bearded man walks up and tells him that there's a meeting in the faculty room. It's Jimmy, his old Carolina classmate. He saunters off to the door marked "Faculty Room".

As I walk away, back down the street lined with *chaiwallahs* and *paan* stains, towards the station, my student friend says, "I wish the music industry here wasn't so goddamned looked down upon. It can be so much more. My parents would never let me pursue it by itself. For them, there has to be a back-up. Which is why I'm trying for a doctorate in genetics. I think Bollywood is half to blame for this image mishap. It demonised the music industry."

A generation of potters

In stark contrast to the 520 acres of crammed space that defines Dharavi, the 22 acres of Kumbharwada seems like a Gujarati village in itself: small houses with sloping roofs, all of which usually open out to a common or a private verandah. Kumbharwada is one of the many community settlements that are components of Dharavi. Jeeniben can be seen relaxing outside in the verandah of the tiny room she calls home, wearing a typical *bandhani* sari and chatting with her daughters-in-law. The two younger women work meticulously at their potter's wheels, a very different sight from other households in Kumbharwada, where it is the men who make the clay pots.

Jeeniben, a 67-year-old mother of two boys lights up whenever someone asks her how the community got its name. "*Kumbhar* or *Kumhar* is a potter and *wada* means a colony, hence the name Kumbharwada—colony of potters," Jeeniben explains. She, along with her husband and father-in-law migrated to Mumbai from Saurashtra after her marriage in 1971.

Kumbharwada is the largest community of potters in Mumbai, housing more than 1,500 families, most of whom still practise the traditional method of pottery. Fed up with the state of affairs in Dharavi that restricted their growth, the countless communities residing there challenged the pitiful state they were in. They rose from their helplessness and found a new way of life. It is the hard work and ingenuity of these families that gives Dharavi its identity today. Jeeniben's is one such family.

In the early 20th century a drought-hit Saurashtra, Gujarat, and 150 to 200 potter families came to Mumbai by sea. Initially after migration, the Kumbhar families were spread out across the city, but the British later allotted them land at the edge of the island city in Dharavi.

In 1932, an inferno gutted all the houses in Kumbharwada, after which the trader community in Mumbai helped the potter families get back on their feet by giving them money, food and shelter.

The communities began setting up small cottage industries of various kinds to sustain themselves. Jeeniben and her family make earthen pots, bowls and *diyas*.

"Here in Kumbharwada, indigenous red and grey clay is used to make pots. We procure the clay from neighbouring cities like Rajkot, Ahmedabad and Thane. This clay is gathered at Bhiwandi and Kalyan and supplied to Kumbharwada," Jeeniben explains. "We bake the moulds in traditional kilns that are placed in our open courtyards and fired using material waste."

She boasts, "We usually manage to make more than 2,000 diyas every day, and Diwali and Sankrant are the most hectic times for us. During off-season people buy these diyas from us wholesale," adds her daughter-in-law Parvati.

Jeeniben and her family share their open courtyard space with a Kutchi Muslim family and maintain an extended family-like relationship with them. "They are like my own children, and they treat me with a great deal of respect!" she says, watching her grandchildren running around with the neighbour's youngsters. Jeeniben recalls the communal tension in the city after the Babri Masjid demolition in 1992. "During those days, my family felt safe only because of our neighbours and their friendship towards us," she says with gratitude.

The Kumbharwada community is very close knit and has a great sense of pride. They have a strong identity of their own and consider themselves independent of the rest of Dharavi. They also consider themselves the owners of the land that they live on. The 28 square metres of land that has been sanctioned by the government as part of the Dharavi Redevelopment Project for each of them is inadequate, but with the existing levels of poverty, it has been impossible for them to acquire more.

Despite all the hardships, Jeeniben doesn't complain. She says, "Mumbai has been very kind to me so far. But still, I do look forward to visiting my village. I love the slow paced life back there. Here, everyone is in a hurry to get somewhere and do something."

When Buddha came to Bombay

Most taxi drivers at Dadar station look perplexed when asked to go to the Japanese Temple. "Where's that? Are you sure you have the right address?" asked one. Another used Google maps to find it. Tucked away in a quiet little pocket of Worli, Nipponzan Myohoji temple is an elegant building of sandstone and marble almost entirely shrouded by the foliage of trees growing around it. If it wasn't for a board with the name outside, it would have been near impossible to find this shrine.

Like any other Japanese temple, Nipponzan Myohoji too has a lush garden around it. There is a stone bench at the entrance, perhaps made for weary travellers. Unlike the busy street that it faces, the plot itself is quiet, the only sounds being the chirping of the birds and rustling leaves in the garden. It is a space for quiet reflection and introspection. A flight of steps leads to a central gathering space used for meditation and prayer. It faces the main shrine which is open and has a pristine white idol of the Buddha. The temple is very simple; its beauty is in its profound simplicity.

Sitting in that space and meditating is unlike meditating anywhere else; there is a direct yet intangible connection with Buddha that I could feel. On asking the caretaker of the temple I was taken to an area behind it to meet Bhikshu Morita, the resident Japanese monk. *Bhikshu* is the word for "male Buddhist monk" in Sanskrit. He was sitting on the steps in a calm, almost meditative state. It was Buddha Jayanti; there was food for visitors. Every once in a while he would look up and make sure that everyone was fed. To my astonishment, he spoke fluent Hindi, albeit with a slight accent.

He called me to to his study which is located to the right of the shrine; to the left are his living quarters. He showed me a folder with articles written about him and the temple in newspapers. He handed me his business card. Again, I was taken aback.

"My father wasn't Buddhist; I chose the path of Buddhism," he said in a staccato. Then he asked me when I was born. He chuckled when I told him. "I came here before you were born," he said. "My Guruji sent me to India in 1976; 38 years have gone by since the time I came here....When I initially came to India from Japan I started a peace march to Punjab with my father." A quick search online told me about Nichidatsu Fujii, known as Fujii Guruji, who founded Nipponzan-Myōhōji-Daisanga, a new religious movement that emerged from the Nichiren sect of Japanese Buddhism. On reading Nichiren's declaration that the Lotus-Sūtra would one day be preached in India, Nichidatsu Fujii decided to come to this country. The temple was built on his request.

"Japanese people still live in Mumbai, but they're mostly businessmen, so they stay for short periods of time. They visit me whenever they come," he said. "My experience here? It has been very good. I am very grateful. The love and reverence people give me is more than enough. I'm content and very happy here," he smiled. He instantly looked younger.

Despite having woken up much earlier than usual for morning prayers and rituals for Buddha Jayanti, he was very cheerful and energetic. He asked me about myself, my background and my hobbies. He told me to wait for a minute and went to another room, emerging with a book written by Fujii Guruji. I thanked him and bowed the way Japanese people do to show respect.

As I waited outside eating a bowl of *kheer* he came out and called me. "You like books, don't you? Take this and read it," he said. When I asked him how much to pay, he just asked me to keep it. It was a book on Buddhism. I thanked him effusively. This experience was interesting and memorable for several reasons; it is one I will always cherish. It was written at the back of the book to return it, donate it or pass it on after reading. The knowledge was meant to be shared.

Finishing my *kheer*, I saw two people nearby who looked Japanese. The man seemed older; the woman with him was probably his daughter. She was wearing earrings which looked like metal turtles with blue jade embedded on the backs. I asked them if they were Japanese. "We're Chinese," the man said. His name was Silin Hu. The girl was his daughter. "I was born and brought up here. My grandparents had come in the 1920s. There was a lot of political unrest in China. In those days you didn't need a visa; all you had to do was pack your bag, buy a ticket and leave. That's how they came here," she explained. "Chinese people came and settled in poorer neighbourhoods of town, mostly slums in Grant Road. There was a Chinese school and a small Chinese temple too. They were destroyed after the Indo-China War. Several Chinese families were deported, which few survived. When Chinese families began to do well financially they moved to different parts of town. That's why there are no Chinese colonies any more. There are very few Chinese families in Mumbai now. There's no Chinatown in Mumbai, unlike in Kolkata. There are many Chinese families in Kolkata. I'm married and I live in Kolkata, that's how I know," she told me. "I spent my childhood in Hubli, but came to Mumbai to study. I've worked here ever since. I'm as much a part of this city as anyone else," she said. After having a short conversation with the Bhikshu, they left.

Mumbai has seen immigrants from countries all across the globe and has given a home to many. These people in their turn carried their traditions and faith forward by building religious institutions in the city. Some of these have been lost in time, but others shelter faiths that burn like the flame of a candle, spreading light. In the early 20th century Mumbai became home to the Japanese. In turn, a Japanese monk called Nichidatsu Fujii gave Mumbai a Japanese Buddhist temple. Like an undying flame, it lives on under the care of Bhikshu Morita, who continues to spread Buddha's message, like he did to me. The temple's doors are open to everyone, providing respite to those who are lost spiritually. It gives people shelter, the way Mumbai once gave it safe haven.

Khaike Paan Banaraswallah!

Remember the 1970s hit song '*Khaikepaan Banaras wallah, khul jaye band akal ka taala...*'? Just like the immortal melodies enjoyed even today, the *paan* tradition too is everlasting. Eating *paan* is much more than just chewing a combination of betel leaf, *supari*, *katha*, *chuna*, *gulkand*, honey-flavoured *elaichi* and other exotic ingredients.

Kaushal K Tiwari, often called the 'millionaire *paanwallah*' runs a shop with his brothers near Kemp's Corner in South Mumbai and is famous not just for his variety of *paan* but also for his friendly nature. "We treat our customers like God. We believe in maintaining friendly relations and always try to provide the best service with pure ingredients." The Tiwari *paanwallahs* have different customer-friends dropping by at different times of the day, ranging from businessmen to ordinary folk, families and college students, for whom the *paan* tradition plays an important part of their routine.

Some customers are so well known that their orders are ready and waiting almost before they arrive at the shop, the *paan* made as they park their cars. It's a routine now to make new friends, chatting, smiling, making sure there's no delay in delivering the order while bonding with them gradually. The *paan* shop is now a landmark and an interactive node where a variety of people from different parts of the city connect. "Once a customer, soon a regular" could be the motto!

Kaushal completed his BSc from Bhavan's College and works at Orbit as a facility manager, apart from making *paan* during the evening. "This *paan* shop was established by my grandfather in the early 1960s and since then is being run by the family." His grandfather came to Mumbai at the age of 17 in search of a job and started from scratch. His hard work and enthusiasm successfully converted the vegetable shop he started into a *paan* shop. "This *paan* shop has laid the foundation for our family, so we are attached to it even today. If it wasn't for this, we would all be working as farmers in our village in Uttar Pradesh." After the patriarch's death the family business split and resulted in the Tiwari *paan* shop run by Kaushal and his three brothers.

"There's no experience that can be a waste. I believe that one should learn from all of it," says Kaushal. Along with communicating with customers and understanding new trends in the market, he also has a website and a Facebook page to advertise and supply *paan* for weddings and other celebrations, along with customer references. With his attachment to his grandfather's legacy, he doesn't fail to innovate and come up with new varieties of *paan* to surprise his customers.

Being the third generation running the *paan* shop and a family business doesn't stop Tiwari from educating his children. "Education is a must if you want to do something in life. My father, who wasn't interested in studying, helped my grandfather with the shop before completing his secondary schooling and later discontinued studying.

He wouldn't let me work at the *paan* shop till I completed my HSC and made sure I did."

Kaushal is happy. "We live in a two-room-kitchen in which four of us stay in one room while the kids and one of our wives stays in the other. We make sure that one wife is always present to take care of the kids and the house, while the others take care of things in the village."

And Mumbai makes him content too. "People here are really friendly and understanding. We enjoy catering to them and watch how different people blend like the different flavours of the *paan*. We'll continue with the tradition, it makes us happy and proud." He's one of the rare people who hasn't turned away from his past even as he looks towards the future.

Down memory lane

Bandra, also known as the Queen of the suburbs was once under Portuguese rule, while the rest of Bombay was run by the Bristish East India Company. It originally consisted of 24 hamlets or *pakhadis* that housed fishermen and farmers, the population dominated by Catholics mixed with Parsis and Bohras who arrived around the turn of the century; the Punjabis and Sindhis merged in later. By the late 1990s Bandra became home to the young creative population, ranging from musicians to designers, a generous dose of foreigners thrown in. Today different layers intertwine, showcasing the transformation from green villages with low buildings to tall, hi-tech glazed structures that merge at the seaside promenade. The variety makes it the new heart of the metropolis.

Pali Hill is one of the oldest settlements of Bandra, originally a jungle filled with snakes and colourful birds that offered a calm, scenic beauty, a place where only the British government's Bombay Presidency officers resided. With the film industry blooming fast, actors started buying land at Pali Hill to build bungalows that still nestle between newly constructed skyscrapers.

Travelling up and down the steep slopes of Pali Hill no one can overlook the traditional yellow bungalow that stands serenely on the zig-zagging road as it diverges downhill. Dulcene recalls spending her childhood among the green jungles of the area as she witnessed Bandra growing. "After my parents split up, my uncle brought my younger brother and me all the way from Mangalore to Mumbai. I was hardly eight years old. Around the age of 12, I was adopted by a Parsi couple named Lashkary, who lived in and ran a Gujarati medium school what is now the yellow bungalow."

The yellow house, originally triple-storied, was owned by Dr Patel; later different floors were rented out and then sold to different families. Dulcene recalls bungalows owned by actors that came up then between the dense trees; now they are tall towers. "These paved roads were originally the *kaccha* roads that we used earlier to cross the jungle," she remembers.

"I loved spending time with nature and people then reared ducks, goats, chickens and turkeys. Everything was quite different in those days!" Over time, Dulcene not only started losing track of her mother tongue and learned a new one, but also started adopting new customs and traditions. "During those days the house was shared by different families who had a common telephone that was a big thing, unlike today when almost anyone and everyone owns private mobile phones."

Home is where the story begins. Like many other families, there was the Ansari family that had its roots in Aligarh in Uttar Pradesh. Their young and enthusiastic son Mobin came to Mumbai to become an actor. With his hard work and passion he managed to step into the film world and worked as a publicity officer, where he executed many successful publicity campaigns for iconic movies like Pakeezah and Mughal-e-Azam; subsequently, he also started writing scripts.

"The telephone was on our floor and Mobin, who had made many contacts in the film industry, would keep getting calls. Every time the telephone rang I would have to pass on the message to him." Dulcene studied at the same school and later became a teacher there, while Mobin was still trying his luck in acting, along with designing posters for hit films like *Howrah Bridge*. "After getting to know each other and with both our families happily accepting our relationship we got married at the Juhu Hotel, after dating for four years."

She recalls how people would anxiously wait to watch the first day first show of any new film. "I remember our first show together was *Deedar*, which we saw at Bandra Talkies; that name is still used as a BEST bus stop name. Those were the days of people showing off their vintage cars and so many social gatherings with actors and actresses!" Playing the radio and sitting together was a daily routine then. Bollywood has changed over the years and with Internet connections one doesn't mind missing out on the first day first show, or even watching a movie with a bunch of friends in the theatre.

"It was around 1980 that some builders forcefully tried to break down the home and from the triple storied structure, we were left with a double storied one. Having the owner strip off a floor, we had to then make amendments in the layout of the house. We continued mending the house and doing all we could to safeguard our home from falling apart; it has been witnessing and experiencing things just like us and will always continue to...!" Dulcene smiles.

Mobin often took her on drives through the fields, cutting through the shaded narrow lanes and the town market along Bazaar

Road; at times they enjoyed the tea at the Taj Mahal hotel. In 1984 Mobin passed away and left Dulcene memories that she continues to live with. They have two sons, one settled abroad who visits often, the other staying with his mother and taking care of her. She does jigsaw puzzles with her grandchildren and enjoys hearing them read stories to her.

With roots in the South and the North merging with Parsi customs, Dulcene has mastered different cooking styles and different languages. Idols from Ganpati to Christ and various *devis* abound in the house that welcomes one and all. After all, this house is where stories began and continue to grow!

Sufi by the bay

The air is heavy with the scent of rose water and incense. It is a late Thursday evening and the little causeway swarming with devotees is awash in the golden light of a fading sun. Floating like a sacred mirage off the Worli coast on an islet is the celebrated dargah of the Sufi saint *peer* Haji Ali. It has always been one of Mumbai's most striking landmarks.

Marvelling the huge entrance foyer of the Dargah Sharief, walking across the marble courtyard, I reach the place where most of the devotees have settled down after paying their respects to the saint. It is the music that's so compelling, coming from the *qawwalkhana,* an open hall flanking the waters of the bay. This is where I hear Rajendra Prasad Jaiswal sing the beautiful *qawwali, "Jab girte hue maine tera naam liya hai, Tab manzil ne wahi badh ke mujhe thaam liya hai...." (Whenever I have fallen I have remembered you and your grace has always saved me.)*

Rajendra is one of the lead singers of the Sikander Shad *qawwal* group, one of the many who perform at the dargah every week. "Thursday is considered to be day for the *peer*, and *qawwalis* are the sacred offerings we make to appease him," Rajendra explains this Sufi art form fused with devotion in the brief break between performances. "Sarkar has called me here and adorned me with the voice. I am just following his orders." His every performance is a manifestation of this blissful spiritual existence; it's not a mere ornamentation when he punctuates his *qawwalis* with the vocal dexterity of *taans,* transcending the listener to the mystical and heightened experience of Sufi music. Moreover, with all the energy infused into the environment, it's a spectacle to watch the group perform.

"It has been 12 years since I started singing with my *ustad* Sikander Shad. Though I came to Mumbai in 1980 from Jaunpur, Uttar Pradesh, it was a mill I had to work in to make ends meet back home. But destiny had other plans," reminisces Rajendra. "After the mill shut down in 1982, I was left jobless. I started looking for alternate methods to sustain myself. That's when I took up a job in an orchestra group. Singing, which has been a simple indulgence since childhood, gave me a job that paid me well to sustain myself at that moment. Our group performed at private parties and small events."

It is at one such event where his orchestra was a participant that Rajendra was spotted by Sikander Shad, an established and empanelled *qawwali* singer at Haji Ali. "He was impressed by my hand on the harmonium and asked me to join his group. Since he showed a lot of confidence in me, I joined. But I was amazed how he could ask a non-Muslim to join his group! Also, I didn't know any *qawwalis* then. But all that didn't matter to *ustad*, he said I had Sarkar's grace. He said every true devotee's prayers are answered by Haji Ali, irrespective of him or her being a Hindu or

Muslim," says Rajendra proudly about his journey from a singer to a believer. "Here I am now, singing in his honour. It feels profound and I am content."

This conversation marks a spirit of secularism and a dictum of faith that is prevalent in the complex. The *peer* is considered a healer and teacher, and many, irrespective of religion, flock to the shrine to seek the blessings and solace from the saint, who is now an inherent part of the city's folklore. Hailing from Bukhara, in the ancient Persian Empire, Haji Ali travelled around the world in the early to mid-15th century and settled in Mumbai to continue his religious works. One of the stories his followers tell describes how after his death on the way to Mecca, his coffin was cast into the sea, as per his wishes. However, it floated back to these shores, becoming stuck in the string of rocky islets just off the shore of Worli. And the Dargah was constructed there.

"The popularity of *qawwali* music is very recent. Sufi singers like Nusrat Fateh Ali Khan and Abida Parveen have made it available mainstream. Also, Sufi music is a highly immersive art form. Here the audience's response and display of emotion is part of the whole experience." Rajendra excuses himself to join his group of eight musicians on a low podium in the pillared court of *qawwalkhana*. As he settles in, the *tabla* and harmonium players start setting their tempos for the next performance. Closing his eyes, Rajendra begins singing, a few unadorned verses, captivating in their simplicity. Slowly he meanders through a mellifluous arrangement of *taans* in an utmost '*Ihteraam*'—a song in respect of the saint—bringing out the innate musicality of the *kalaam*. All dressed in white with their heads covered in honour of *peer* Haji Ali, the instrumentalists and chorus join Rajendra, the group becoming a single entity

The *alaaps* are repeated over and over, and often Ustad Sikandar Shad inserts a note or two, pausing to emphasise the last words of each *kalaam* in such a way that the desperation and intense longing of the poet is apparent when he sings, *"Jab dard diya tum ne, phir tum hi dawaa.......karna!"* (*If you have given the suffering, you are the one who will heal it.*)

As the tempo increases, an enraptured crowd of devotees responds with unabashed displays of emotion. The cool breeze from the sea blows in, making the music resound, until everyone present has elevated to a state of spiritual ecstasy...*fanaah*!

Cinderella in khaki

Pramila Kshirsagar, resident of Ahmednagar, is the woman sub-inspector of the Gamdevi Police station next to Kamathipura, one of the most ill-reputed areas of Mumbai. "I am a trainee here, and am studying to be a DYSP (Deputy Superintendent of Police). I was posted here from Ahmednagar, and I passed my exams from Madhya Pradesh. When I got married my husband, a software engineer, followed me to set up base in Mumbai," says Pramila, sitting in her plush office, a startling contrast to the popular image of a *thana*, or police station, with its peeling paint and crumbling facade.

As one of the oldest neighbourhoods of the city, the area has been witness to a number of cases important in the criminal history of the city, with its infamous "cages" and derelict *chawl* buildings abutting the core commercial hub. It sets the mood to a series of paradoxes that become part of the conversation with the young policewoman in her neatly pressed khaki uniform. Pramila was posted here two and half years ago.

"I have a shift from 8am to 8pm. At times, during emergencies, I have to stay back nights at the *thane*. I entered the police force because I lived in poverty and there was no family to support me. After a gruelling training period, I attained this post. However, I have further ambitions, of being a DYSP." Pramila has six cases to deal with, ranging from theft to gang robberies. She seems fearless and nonchalant as she talks about them. She is one of the large Mumbai police team, a group often misread as being corrupt and with minimum educational qualifications. On the contrary, these guardians of the law have passed their main civil service examinations. They are also considered to be one of the best police forces of the country, credited for the remarkable decline in crime rates in the district over the years.

"As a girl, I was wary of violence. I have never raised my hand on anyone. I remember the first time I gave a thrashing to someone. She was a woman who refused to acknowledge her robbery. My hand wavered, yet I was able to beat a confession out of her," Pramila says, burying all charges of women being the weaker sex. "Along with my work, I also manage my family. I cook in the morning and leave; my husband takes care of the other chores." She is the natural home-maker and the tough cop all in one garb, an inspirational contradiction to the stereotypical image of Indian women.

For many, being born a woman into an Indian household entails responsibilities. It involves knowing that at a certain period in your life you will have to manage your household and be submissive to your in-laws. It also involves knowing that irrespective of the time of day that you go out, you have to be extra careful of lecherous men who roam the streets.

And then there are the accusations that may be levelled against you about your being the weaker sex, the one physically incapable of tough labour, and the one whose nature, by virtue of birth, is supposed to be demure and motherly. There are so many burdens heaped on the shoulders of the Indian woman that it is refreshing to see a woman of valour take apart these pre-conceived notions and grind them to dust.

"I have faced no discrimination at work. I handle women-related cases as well as hardcore male criminals. There are no gender skews as such," Pramila insists, with tacit reference to the recent case in Mumbai of a woman constable being molested on a bus by the conductor. Police stations, ironically, are not the safest of places either. There have been issues of rape happening in police stations, of incessant beatings of innocent people by policemen. Pramila maintains that she hasn't experienced any such atrocities yet.

All through the *thane* we see a changing dynamic. New cases are being handled by women constables who usher in attendees and criminals alike. A woman cop handles the interrogation of a man in a room. It is not uncommon to see woman beat-marshalls dressed in their khaki pantsuits with their hair worn up in a stark no-nonsense bun patrolling the streets after dark. These are modern Indian women who refuse to acknowledge the weight on their shoulders and approach the world with a confidence and stature that is refreshing.

Once upon a time Indian women were supposed to keep their heads covered and look at strangers through latticework (*jaali*) or be in *purdah*. Today, the tradition continues in a new form; the woman of now must look at people through the *purdah* of suspicion and mistrust.

These are women who grew up in tough training camps, learned martial arts and the fine arts of negotiation. These are women who recognise that pre-conceived notions are baseless metaphors, that in this world they are as strong as they choose to be. Pramila joins ranks with her male counterparts without insecurity or trepidation, and she is the one who will hopefully usher in a new gender parity in a fresh new world.

215

Working for the Raja

It's August rain in Mumbai. Though it's not the typical cats-and-dogs kind, the clogged drains have resulted in overflow onto the road, with the occasionally moving traffic splashing muck further around. But all this does not seem to deter the enthusiasm of the endlessly long queue of devotees, all barefoot, waiting with garlands, sweets and offerings, occasionally bursting into "*Ganpati bappa morya*". Patiently they wait their turn to visit the most famous *Ganpati mandal* in Mumbai—Lalbaug*cha Raja*.

"Often the queues are four or five kms long. It is intense devotion and a deep belief that motivates all these people to come here every year. They know that *Bappa* answers their prayers. Which is why he is also called *navascha* (wishgranter) *Ganpati*," says Amol Parte, one of the key volunteers, trying to explain the phenomenon. "This one began as a small *mandal* made by the *kolis,* the local fishing community, here in the Peru Compound in 1928, a few years after Lokmanya Tilak, a renowned national leader, began the celebration as a means of community engagement during the freedom movement."

217

Over the past 74 years it has grown immensely popular and so large in scale, that there is now a core committee of 35 members who work all through the year to ensure that the event sails along smoothly, with the support of over 1,200 volunteers. "Right from managing the different kind of queues to facilitating the devotees' food, water and services, the tasks are assigned and divided between us all. Along with religious feelings, it is a spirit of community and social service which motivates us all to work for *Raja*," says Amol, who was born and brought up in the neighbourhoods of Lalbaug and Parel.

"Every aspect of the work here is elaborate." Being in a dense suburb with a dearth of space, a lot of planning is required, from building multiple makeshift shelters and bridges for the devotees to making and installing the 12-foot-tall idol. "For 50 years Venkatesh Kamble and now his nephew Santosh Kamble have been making the idol. The ornamentation that you see are offerings; however, the simplicity is that the idol is the same every year. They have used the same mould for the last 50 years; it has been patented as well. But beyond just organising the event, the committee has a vision for the local community; Sudhir Salvi has spearheaded and ensured this," Amol explains the philanthropic vision. "We have set up a free library and a couple of computer knowledge institutions to enable youth and provide them with vocational training. The *mandal* also runs a dialysis centre for a nominal fee, along with providing medical funds to needy patients in a few government hospitals in the city."

With technology embracing the logistics of their event—surveillance cameras, intercom systems, an almost-corporate working of the *mandal*—Amol observes how the history and development of his locality overlaps with the evolution of the *mandal*.

"Lalbaug has been an area of *kaamgar* (working class) with the maximum mills in the area. Back then, when many migrated from the interiors of Maharashtra and Gujarat to work in the mills, the landlords provided *chawls* and schools close to the work place. People did not have to travel beyond 1.5 km for anything, but only 25 per cent of the population was educated. Subsequently, when the mills shut down, the crime rate went higher. I remember, in my growing up years there was a lot of discrimination we faced from the upmarket Dadar residents. Even in schools, students from Parel and Byculla areas were not admitted," recalls Amol, who has studied automobile engineering, about the lack of mobility and education which for decades hampered the growth in the area.

"Over the past two decades the thinking has been evolving. Education has played a huge role. We also look at the redevelopment of these areas as a hope for better facilities. Unlike our elders who thought that the builders were here to swindle us, education and political consciousness has armed us with abilities to negotiate for our betterment," says Amol representing a new wave of entrepreneurship. "Now everyone is thinking beyond the 'job mentality' and a few are coming forward as entrepreneurs. After working for Mahindra & Mahindra Ltd. for a couple of years, I decided to take up real estate. It is far more fulfilling to be my own boss. It also gives me time to follow my political interests; I actively work and support a local party: MNS."

So is it political aspirations that motivate him to work for the *mandal?* He is quick to deny this. "Working for Lalbaug*cha* Raja is an honour; it's social work. The people involved in the work belong to different political banners. However, under the umbrella of *Bappa,* we are all united. You will not find a single political hoarding

219

or flag on the premises. *Bappa* connects us all! It is a message for all people who are divided by caste, creed and community."

He elaborates by adding that on the 10th day, the procession that is taken out to immerse the idol is one of the longest in the city. "It passes through the old town, through the old Gujarati and Mohammedan districts of CP Tank, Do Tanki and Agripada and finally reaches Girgaum after 22 hours. The belief in the deity is so strong that without any barriers of religion, people flock to pay their respect during the procession."

Girgaum Chowpatty and the other beaches in the city are chock-a-block with tourists, devotees, volunteers during the final days of the puja. Watching over a sea of people, idols from all over the city are immersed in the sea in one of the biggest spectacles Mumbai has to offer. Lalbaug*cha* Raja is supposed to be the last idol in the city to be immersed, marking the end of the 10-day-long festivity. *Ganesha* or *Ganpati,* the Hindu god of wisdom and luck, bids adieu to his devotees, promising to visit with the same grandeur the next year.

Glossary

Aai mother, in Marathi.

Alaap a term used in Indian classical music, meaning the free flow of the *Raga*, in which there are no words and no fixed rhythm. It is the purest form of melody.

Adda, an informal place where a group of people gather or hang out, in Hindi.

Adivasi an umbrella term used for a heterogeneous set of ethnic and tribal groups considered to be the aboriginal population of India.

Akshay Kumar a popular Indian film actor, producer and martial artist.

Amitabh Bachchan a popular Bollywood actor.

Arrey baap re an expression in Hindi meaning "Oh my God!", often used to show surprise.

Azan the Islamic call to the ritual prayer called *namaaz* (see *namaaz*) made by a *muezzin* from the minaret of a mosque, in Urdu.

Bal mela literally, children's fair. Part of the rural and urban landscape in India, it is a fun and frolic with rides and activities for children and stalls for games, food and exhibitions and performances when conducted on a larger scale.

Baba father, in Marathi.

Baida eggs, also called "*andaa*", in Hindi.

Bandhani sari *sari* is a long traditional garment worn by Indian women, draped around the body. *Bandhani*, a Hindi word meaning "tie", is a particular type of *sari* made by using a tie-and-dye technique in states of Rajasthan and Gujarat in India.

Bappa Hindu god Ganpati is fondly called, in Marathi (see Ganpati).

Bazaar market, in Hindi.

Berimbau a single-string percussion musical instrument, a musical bow, from Brazil.

Bhai brother, in Hindi.

Bhajan Hindu devotional songs (see Hindu).

Bhelwallah the seller of *bhelpuri*, often referred to as *bhel*, a mouth-watering savoury Indian *chaat (see chaat)* made of puffed rice, vegetables and a tangy tamarind sauce.

Bhurji spicy scrambled egg dish.

Bohra Muslim also known as Dawoodi Bohra, belonging to a sub-sect of Shia Islam and tracing their belief system back to Yemen.

Brunmaska literally, bread butter. '*Brun*' is a local bread that is crisp, hard and crumbly on the outside and soft inside and '*maska*' means butter. It is an Iranian dish and a must-have with tea at Irani cafes in Mumbai.

Buddha Jayanti a celebration of the birth of Buddha, his enlightenment and death, or the attainment of *Nirvana*.

Chaat Hindi, describing lip-smacking savoury snacks typically served on pavements in the evening, at stalls or food carts in various public spaces like beaches.

Chacha Nehru or Jawaharlal Nehru, the first Prime Minister of India, referred to as *Chacha* (Uncle in Hindi) Nehru because of his love for children.

Chaiwallah Hindi, literally meaning a tea seller.

Chawl a low-income housing typology, usually four to five stories high, with 10–20 tenements flanking long corridors. Many *chawls* were constructed in the early 1900s to house people migrating to Mumbai as mill workers.

Chikoo pulpy brown fruit of a long-lived evergreen tree.

Chor thief, in Hindi.

Chuna slaked lime, in Hindi.

Coolie in Hindi, usually a porter working on daily wages, wearing a typical red and white uniform with a white *topi* (see *topi*) and a license plate tied on the upper arm.

Dabbawallah also spelled *dabbawalla* or *dabbawala*; people, most commonly in Mumbai, who are part of a delivery system that collects, delivers and returns lunchboxes for working people who choose the luxury of home-made food.

Dadi paternal grandmother, in Hindi.

Dakhma or *dokhma,* also known as "Tower of Silence" is a circular structure used by Parsi Zoroastrians as part of the ritual of parting with the dead.

Dal chawal "dal" means lentils and "chawal" means rice, in Hindi. It is the staple food in most parts of North India.

Dargah an Islamic shrine built over the grave of a revered religious figure, often a Sufi saint or dervish.

Darshan an opportunity to see or an occasion of seeing a holy person or the image of a deity in a temple, in Hindi.

Devi goddesses, in Hindi.

Devi puja in Hindi, meaning to offer prayers or worship the goddess. The ritual consists of singing *bhajans* and *aarti* (see *bhajan).*

Deedar a 1951 Bollywood classic.

223

Dhansak is a Parsi Zoroastrian delicacy, a thick meat and lentil-based curry usually eaten with rice.

Dilwale Dulhania Le Jayenge or DDLJ, a 1995 Indian romantic drama film revolving around the characters Raj and Simran who meet on a trip to Europe. After initial misadventures, they fall in love and the battle begins to win over two traditional families. Considered an ode to love by many, DDLJ still runs every day in its 20th year at Mumbai's iconic Maratha Mandir Theatre.

Diwali or *Deepawali,* is a Hindu festival of lights, held between October and November. *"Deep"* means light and *"awali"* means a row. People clean their homes and decorate it with lights or *diyas* (see *diya*) before Diwali. During the festival, they wear new clothes, light fireworks and worship and welcome *Lakshmi,* the goddess of prosperity. According to legend, Diwali commemorates the return of Lord Rama, king of Ayodhya along with Sita, his wife, and Lakshman, his brother, from a 14-year-long exile and the defeat of the demon-king Ravana.

Diya oil lamp, usually made from clay, with a cotton wick dipped in *ghee* or vegetable oil, in Hindi.

Dungchen a long trumpet or horn used in Tibetan and Mongolian Buddhist ceremonies.

Dupatta in Hindi, a long scarf that is a part of ethnic attire of women in northern India, the *salwar-kameez.*

Durgapuja also referred to as *Durgotsava* or *Sharadotsav,* an annual Hindu festival that is dedicated to the on worship of the goddess Durga. It is celebrated with great pomp and show in the state of West Bengal.

Elaichi cardamom, in Hindi.

Fanaah the Sufi term for "passing away" or "annihilation" (of the self).

Ferrywallah a person who drives a boat or ship for conveying passengers and goods, especially over a relatively short distance and as a regular service.

Gadda mattress, bed cushion, large padded cushion, etc., in Hindi

Ganji traditional vest worn by men.

Gajra string of flowers.

Ganpati A Hindu god of wisdom and luck, the elephant God, also called Ganesha.

Ganpati Bappa Morya an expression to praise Ganpati, in Marathi, praying for his return the next year to shower his blessings.

Gharwali female owner/head of the house, wife, in Hindi.

Gulkand rose jelly used as an ingredient in *paan* (see *paan*), in Hindi.

Hindutva meaning "Hindu-ness", an ideology that sought to define Indian culture in terms of Hindu values. It is the prominent movement advocating Hindu nationalism in India.

Holi the Indian festival of colours. The legend of this celebration revolves around more than one story—the soul bond of Lord Krishna and Radha, Prahlad, the child-devotee of Lord Vishnu, Kamdeva, the Indian Cupid-God and Dhundhi, the immortal ogress.

Ihteraam an Urdu, Arabic or Persian word meaning respect.

Jamun Syzygiumcumini, or jamun, is the fruit of an evergreen tropical tree that is often used to make a purple vegetable dye.

Jhunka bhakar a staple food of the rural population of Maharashtra. Although known as poor man's food, it is definitely rich in flavour and nutrients. *Jhunka* is a spicy preparation of gram flour and onions, while *bhakri* is a round flat unleavened bread/roti made of a mixture of different flours.

Kaccha road an unpaved road made organically over the land that it passes through, in Hindi.

Kalaam verse, in Urdu.

Kamathis a community that has historically engaged in manual labour, originally from Andhra Pradesh.

225

Kamgaar working class, in Marathi.

Kanda onions, in Hindi.

Kapda cloth, in Hindi.

Katha catechu, used as an ingredient in *paan* (see *paan*).

Khaala aunt, in Urdu.

Khaike paan Banaras wallah... a song from the famous action-thriller movie *Don* starring Amitabh Bachchan, released in 1978 and remade in 2006 with Shah Rukh Khan. The first line literally translates to "Eating a *paan* from Benares opens the lock of an idle mind" (see *paan, Amitabh Bachchan*).

Kheemapav minced mutton cooked with onions, garlic, tomatoes, chillies and spices, served with "*pav*" (see *pav*). It is a popular street food, and the best *kheemapav* can be found at Mohammad Ali Road, Mumbai.

Kheer a delicious sweet pudding made by boiling rice, broken wheat, tapioca, or vermicelli with milk and sugar; it is flavoured with cardamom, saffron and dry fruit.

Konkani a linguistic community from the Konkan coast of western India.

Kurta a long upper garment for men and women, with regional variations of form in length, style, material and design.

Kutchi Muslim a Muslim community of Pakistan and India, the original residents of the Kutch region of the western state of Gujarat.

Lathi in Hindi, a long, heavy iron-bound bamboo stick used as a weapon by the police in India.

Losar the Tibetan word for the new year. "*Lo*" means year, age; "*sar*" means new, fresh. It is a three-day festival that mixes sacred and secular practices—prayers, ceremonies, prayer flags, sacred and folk dancing and partying. Losar is the most important holiday in Tibet, Nepal and Bhutan.

Lotus-Sūtra one of the most important and influential *Mahāyāna sutras* or sacred scriptures, on the basis of which the Tiantai and Nichiren schools of Buddhism were established.

Luchi Bengali for *puri* (see *puri*).

Luck a 2009 Hindi action-thriller film directed and written by Soham Shah.

Maacher jhol fish curry, in Bengali, where *"maacher"* means fish and *"jhol"* means curry. Traditionally served with steamed rice, it is a delicacy in West Bengal.

Mahajan an Indian surname or title originally given to those who are believed to be descendants of the Gupta dynasty who migrated from Maharashtra and Madhya Pradesh to Rajasthan and then to Punjab several hundred years ago. Over the years, the word *Mahajan* has become a generic job title used to describe people involved in money lending.

Maidan a large open space or ground used for parades or public meetings, in Hindi. Shivaji Park in Dadar is one such place in Mumbai.

Mandala temporary structure built especially during the 10-day-long Ganesh festival for housing the idol; a committee of people overseeing the celebrations during Ganesh festival (also called Ganesh utsav).

Mandir a Hindu temple.

Mantra Sanskrit, meaning a word or sound repeated to aid concentration in meditation, a Vedic hymn originally in Hinduism and Buddhism.

Mumbaikar a resident of Mumbai, in Marathi.

Mumbaiyya a Hindi word meaning of or belonging to Mumbai.

Mumba Devi goddess Mumba, the local incarnation of Devi (see *Devi*) from whom Mumbai derives its name.

Namaaz the ritual prayers prescribed by Islam, in Urdu, ideally to be observed five times a day.

Nichirensect Nichiren Buddhism or Hokkeshu is a branch of Mahāyāna Buddhism based on the Lotus Sutra (see *Lotus Sutra*) and an attendant belief that all people have an innate Buddha nature and are therefore inherently capable of attaining enlightenment in their current form and present lifetime.

Onam the harvest festival in Kerala celebrated with great joy and enthusiasm by people of all communities. It marks the homecoming of the legendary King Mahabali.

Paan a Hindi word for the betel leaf, traditionally completing the Indian meal. The quintessential *paan* has been around for generations in its fascinating varieties, an important part of social life and customs for many years in India. In the courts of the Moghul kings, *paan* was chewed as a palate cleanser and breath freshener, and offered as a gesture of hospitality, friendship and love.

Paanwallah literally, betel leaf seller in Hindi. In India, a *paan*-seller is found in every nook and corner of cities, towns and villages.

Paisa a monetary unit of India, Pakistan, and Nepal, equal to one hundredth of a rupee. Also means money in spoken Hindi.

Pagdi system a kind of local traditional semi-ownership property deal. In this system the tenant can buy semi-ownership rights from the landlord, but the latter still has a say and shares profits in the re-selling or renting of the property. It is an informal deposit system where the landlord tends to run the show.

Papad or *papadum* in Tamil is celebrated in a well-known Indian tongue twister—*Kachapapad, pakkapapad.* It is a thin, round wafer, sometimes described as a cracker or flatbread, served as an accompaniment to an Indian meal, as a snack or as croutons in soups. *Papads* (Hindi) are made of black gram or other dried lentils, eaten fried or roasted. The dough is traditionally dried in the sun and can be cooked by deep-frying, roasting over an open flame, toasting or microwaving, depending on the desired texture.

Patra corrugated tin sheet used to secure a site under construction, in Hindi.

Pav a kind of Indian bread. Pav means a small loaf of bread, a word derived from *pão*—a Portuguese word for bread. The Portuguese brought yeast to India, which produced the paired loaves. Indians started calling these double bread or *pav.*

Paya goat's trotter soup, a traditional Muslim dish served during festivals.

Peer title for a Sufi master in Urdu. They are also referred to as Hazrat or Shaikh, which is Arabic for old man. The title is often translated into English as "saint".

Prasad a portion of food, mainly sweets or fruits that is given as a religious offering to deities in Hinduism. It is distributed to devotees after the *puja* (see *puja*).

Pukka homes dwellings that are designed to be solid and permanent, built of stone, brick, concrete or timber.

Puri a small round piece of bread made of unleavened wheat flour, deep-fried and served with meat or vegetables. A popular choice of breakfast in India is *puri-bhaji*, puri served with vegetables, usually potato.

Pyaar love, in Hindi.

Qalam a word in Urdu, Hindi and Persian, derived from Greek, traditionally meaning a pen made from a dried reed, used for Islamic calligraphy.

Qalamkari or *"Kalamkari"* is a type of hand-painted or block-printed cotton fabric produced in parts of India and Iran.

Qawwal a person who sings *qawwali.*

Qawwali a word in Urdu, in India and Pakistan, is an energetic musical performance of Sufi Muslim poetry that aims to lead listeners to a state

229

of religious ecstasy, to a spiritual union with Allah. It is devotional and expresses love for and oneness with God, traditionally sung by a group of men to the accompaniment of musical instruments.

Rakhi traditionally a cotton thread bracelet, typically bearing elaborate ornamentation, tied on the Indian festival of Raksha Bandhan by a girl or woman on the wrist of her brother or someone she considers one, asking for lifelong protection from him. The brother in turn gives a gift to his sister, as an assurance of fulfilling this duty.

Ramgarh ke Sholay a 1991 Bollywood feature film that parodies the 1975 classic Bollywood blockbuster *Sholay*.

Ramakrishna Mission an organisation which forms the core of a worldwide spiritual movement known as the Ramakrishna Movement or the Vedanta Movement. The mission conducts extensive work in health care, disaster relief, rural management, tribal welfare, elementary and higher education and culture.

Rotis thin, flat Indian bread made from whole wheat flour traditionally known as *atta*. It is a staple food of North Indians.

Sabzi refers to a vegetable or a mix of many vegetables cooked in oil with spices and generally eaten with rice or *rotis*.

Sankrant or Makar Sankranti an important Hindu festival celebrated with kite-flying and sweet savories.

Shagird a pupil, student or disciple, in Urdu.

Sahib a respectful title used for a master or superior. Originally an Arabic word, now used commonly in Hindi and Urdu.

Salliboti a delicious, famous and well-loved Parsi dish. It gets its name from "*salli*", meaning sticks, for the potato sticks in it, and "*boti*", which means chunks of meat.

Sarkaar the man in authority, chief. It is used by Sufis to refer to the Almighty.

Sarpanch an elected head of a village-level statutory institution of local self-government called the *panchayat*.

Shaakha or *shaakha-pola* in Bengali and *chooda* in Punjabi, a set of ivory and red wax/lac bangles worn by women as a sign of marriage.

Shravan the fifth month in the Hindu calendar, beginning in late July and ending in the third week of August.

Sheeshee an expression of disgust in Hindi.

Shukravaar Hindi for the sixth day of the week, i.e., Friday.

Sorpotel or *Sarapatel* is a dish of Portuguese origin, now a delicacy commonly cooked in the coastal Konkan region of India, primarily Goa or Mangalore and by the East Indians of Mumbai.

Supari arecanut, in Hindi. It is an ingredient used in *paan* (see *paan*).

Taans a virtuoso technique used in the vocal performance of a *raga* in Hindustani classical music; an improvised vocal or instrumental musical phrase.

Tabela cowshed in Hindi.

Tabla a drum set used in Indian classical music. It comprises of the *dagga* (bass drum) and the *tabla* (treble drum).

Talav pond, lake or any small water body, in Hindi and Marathi.

Thana police station, in Hindi and Marathi.

Thekedaar a small-time contractor in Hindi. He is responsible for providing labour and materials for construction.

Topi Hindi, meaning cap or hat. There are many types of *topis* worn by different communities in India, for example, the white *topi* worn by men in Maharashtra or the crochet *topi* often worn by Muslim men during prayers.

Upma a traditional breakfast dish or popular snack in the southern part of India and Maharashtra, made from semolina or *suji*, considered to

231

be light and healthy. *Upma* is served with coconut chutney, yoghurt or lime pickle.

Ustad Urdu or Persian word used as an honorific title for well-regarded teachers and artistes, most often musicians, especially in Indian classical music.

Vadapav or *wada pav/pao*, not be confused with the South Indian *wada*. It is a popular fast food dish native to the state of Maharashtra, with a deep fried, batter-coated potato fritter sandwiched into a *pav* (see *pav*).

Varanbhaat Marathi word for lentil-rice, where "*varan*" means lentil curry or stew or "*dal*" and "*bhaat*" means steamed rice. It is integral to Maharashtrian and Goan cuisines and is offered to Lord Ganesha during the Ganesh Chaturthi festival.

Visarjan a word in Sanskrit meaning the immersion of idols in water as an act of respectfully bidding adieu to the deity on the final day of a festival such as Ganesh Chaturthi or Durga Puja. It is celebrated with great vigour in India, when the streets are buzzing with loud music, colours and dancing faces of joy.

Warli *Warli* or *Varli* is an indigenous tribe or *adivasis* (see *adivasi*) living in mountainous and coastal areas along the Maharashtra-Gujarat border. Their style of painting is famous for the unique style depicting their community and life.

Xacuti a curry native to Goa, usually made with chicken or lamb. It is known as *chacuti* in Portuguese.

Zindaggi Rocks a 2006 Bollywood film directed by Tanuja Chandra about the love story between a famous singer and a doctor, and the sacrifice of a mother for her child.

Abbreviations

BEST Bombay Electrical Supply and Transport, the bus transport system of Mumbai and a ferry service in the northern reaches of the city.

BJP Bharatiya Janata Party, or Indian People's party, which espouses Hindu nationalism. The current Prime Minister of India, Narendra Modi belongs to the BJP.

BMC Bombay Municipal Corporation, the civic body that governs the city of Mumbai, the richest municipal organisation in India.

BPO Business Process Outsourcing, a subset of outsourcing that involves the contracting of the operations and responsibilities of specific business functions (or processes) to a third-party service provider.

BPT Bombay Port Trust, an autonomous corporation owned by the Government of India that administers the Bombay Port, primarily used for bulk cargo. Most container traffic is directed to NhavaSheva port across the harbour.

HSC Higher Secondary Examination is a centralised examination for class XII students in India and Nepal.

IMDb the Internet Movie Database, an online database of information related to films, television programmes and video games, detailing

233

actors, production crews, fictional characters, biographies, plot summaries and trivia.

MAMI Film Festival the Mumbai Academy of the Moving Image or MAMI is a public trust that organises the annual international film festival in Mumbai, known as the Mumbai Film Festival (MFF).

MMRDA Mumbai Metropolitan Regional Development Authority is a body of the Government of Maharashtra responsible for the infrastructure development of the Mumbai Metropolitan Region since 1975. It is the richest state-owned organisation in India.

MNS Maharashtra Navnirman Sena is a Maharashtrian Nationalist party based in Maharashtra, led by politician Raj Thackerey.

RSS Rashtriya Swayamsevak Sangh, literally meaning National Volunteer Organisation or National Patriotic Organisation, is a charitable, educational, right-wing volunteer Hindu nationalist group. RSS states that its ideology is based on the principle of selfless service to the nation.

Authors

	Mariel Drego marieldrego@gmail.com	A tale of two ticket*wallahs* The duplicate A universal escape strategy Circulating happiness	Sounds of change No laughing matter The fleeting resident Ups and downs
	Ipshita Karmakar ipshitakarmakar2212@gmail.com	Dalalstreet.com The land of the *vadapav* Through the prayer flags Towers of silence	Synapses within The road less taken Married to the city Cinderella in khaki
	Caleb Pereira calebpereira9123@gmail.com	"I think better when I run" Master of a few arts Torrents of reel Behind the scenes	The scion Carving a niche The wordsmith It's so not Bollywood!
	Krupa Shah krupa34.ks@gmail.com	Always have a Plan B Many fractions, one community Making a difference Dream.Believe. Achieve	Whispers children shouldn't hear A generation of potters Addicted Little things in life

Sachi Mavinkurve sachi.mavinkurve@ gmail.com	Great depths The boy called theatre Fishy business The fading *brun maska*	It's play time When Buddha came to Bombay From mills to the sky
Vanessa Lobo Vanessa.lobo93@gmail. com	Coolie no. 1035 The invisible visible A prolonged holiday Next station: Nallasopara	Mujawar's travels *Khaike paan banaraswallah*! Old is gold! Down memory lane
Aarsha Raveendran aarshar@gmail.com	Past perfect Help for self-help	The Hive
Sahil Dagli sahildagli@hotmail.com	Marathon wings Of bats, balls and bets	
Saman Quraishi vivid.ar08@gmail.com	Sufi by the bay	
Qurratul Ain Contractor qurratulainc@gmail. com	Khaala	
Nisha Nair-Gupta nairnisha2306@gmail. com	Working for the Raja	

About the workshop

"People called Mumbai" was the title of a summer internship held in May 2014. Modelled like a writing workshop, it had five interns from various architecture colleges in Mumbai, and was held across three weeks. In the first week, the interns exhaustively travelled across the city, engaging in numerous conversations and collecting stories. The next two weeks were dedicated to writing, facilitated by a workshop conducted by Nishita Periera. At the end of the workshop, 27 stories about Mumbaikars were penned down. As a greater number of internship applications poured in and ambitions soared, the project was extended by two months. Overall, this book has 10 authors. Out of more than 80 stories, 55 have been shortlisted in the fabulous attempt that is People Called Mumbai.